CW01095949

Advance Praise for
Once Upon a Cove Christmas

"*Once Upon a Cove Christmas* is an engaging read that wraps the reader in the textures, aromas, and cozy beauty of Christmas in a small town on Long Island, New York's North Fork. This second novel in the Lavender Hill Cove series follows a grieving widow who finds solace in faith, family and community while encountering mystery and romance—and maybe even a Christmas miracle. A holiday 'must read!'"

~Kristina Van Kirk, President,
Palm Springs Writers Guild and Screenwriter,
Persephone, The Box, and
Stay Where You Are and Nobody Gets Hurt

"Maryann Ridini Spencer weaves a Christmas holiday tale of love, rivalry, human errors, and reconciliation set against the backdrop of the small village of Lavender Hill Cove. Romantic competitors, juvenile offenders, and village leaders come together to rise above their flaws, awakening to a deeper understanding of the essence of Christmas in their community. There is a message in her words to be cherished by her readers."

~Father Gregory Elder, Ph.D., Pastor,
Sacred Heart Church, Palm Desert, CA

"Lavender Hill Cove, a New England village, is decorated in holiday splendor, and Ella Martin is captivated by the magic of this most wonderful season of the year. But everyone doesn't feel the magic or understand it. Vandals are destroying holiday scenes. But who? And why? So, the mystery begins, and as it unfolds, recently widowed Ella unexpectedly discovers she can fall in love again. *Once Upon a Cove Christmas* is a beautiful holiday story of love, redemption, and second chances. You'll tell your friends about this one!"

~Joanne Hardy, author,
The Girl in the Butternut Dress,
Random Truths, and *ABANDONED*

"When vandals wreak havoc, destroying holiday displays in the charming seaside town of Lavender Hill Cove, Ella and her detective sister, Julie, tackle the mystery. A captivating 'who-done-it' spiced with romance, intrigue, and a little angelic magic, *Once Upon a Cove Christmas* delivers all the requisites for a delightful and insightful Christmas story."

~Rachel Druten, author of nine historical romances for Barbour Publishing and writer and illustrator of the award-winning *Hazel Flick* series

"As the Christmas season approaches and vandalism on local businesses dampens holiday spirits, Ella and her business partner, Sophia, dream up an event to reclaim the season's joy. Meanwhile, Ella and her detective sister, Julie, work to discover who's behind the crimes. *Once Upon a Cove Christmas*, the second novel in the Lavender Hill Cove series mixes intrigue, romance, and a little holiday magic to recapture the true spirit of Christmas in this insightful and engaging novel."

~D. Marie Fitzgerald, author of
A Perfect World, I Have Pictured Myself for Years, F&G,
and *The Love Song*

Other Books by

Maryann Ridini Spencer

Kate Grace novels

Lady in the Window
The Paradise Table
Secrets of Grace Manor
Under the Tropical Skies

Lavender Hill Cove novels

Lavender Hill Cove

Cookbooks

Simply Delicious Living with Maryann®—Entrées

Non-Fiction

Country Skies: Prayerful Bible Meditations for
Morning & Evening
(as K.G. Stevens Photography)

Once Upon a Cove Christmas

Once Upon a Cove Christmas

a Lavender Hill Cove novel

Maryann Ridini Spencer

Santa Rosa©
P R E S S
SantaRosaPress.net

Once Upon a Cove Christmas
First Edition, copyright © 2024
Maryann Ridini Spencer

Hardcover, trade paperback, and eBook editions published in 2024 by Santa Rosa Press®, publisher@SantaRosaPress.net.
Hardcover ISBN: 978-1-7362111-8-2
Paperback ISBN: 978-1-7362111-9-9
eBook/EPUB ISBN: 979-8-9889721-4-3
Library of Congress Control Number: 2024946772

Library of Congress Cataloging-in-Publication Data

Names: Spencer, Maryann Ridini, author.
Title: Once upon a Cove Christmas / Maryann Ridini Spencer.
Series: a Lavender Hill Cove novel

Description: La Quinta, CA; Santa Rosa Press, 2024.
Identifiers: LCCN: 2024946772 | ISBN: 978-1-7362111-8-2 (hardcover) | 978-1-7362111-9-9 (paperback) | 979-8-9889271-4-3 (ebook)

Subjects: LCSH Friendship—Fiction. | Sisters—Fiction. | Family—Fiction. | Christmas—Fiction. | New York (State)—Long Island—Fiction. | Love stories. | Mystery fiction. | BISAC FICTION / Romance / Holidays | FICTION / Christmas | FICTION / Mystery & Detective / Cozy / General | FICTION / Mystery & Detective / Women Sleuths | FICTION / Romance / Christian Fiction / Contemporary | FICTION / Visionary & Metaphysical | FICTION / Women

Classification: LCC PS3619.P4655 O53 2024 | DDC 813.6--dc23

Book Graphics:

House image—Book Cover and Home Sweet Home Title Page—©Adobe Stock, Luxurious Shingle-Style Home with Coastal Charm by Zachary

Scene Breaks—Adobe Stock: Christmas star icon. Christmas tree tip—Vector illustration By lar01joka; Bethlehem north star shape. Clipart image isolated on white and black background.

Title Art—Adobe Stock: Christmas bell. Cozy boho bells clipart. Watercolor illustration. Generative AI. Detailed illustration. By Studicon; Red bird Cardinal on the cedar branch with cones and holly berries Symbol of Christmas, Watercolor hand drawn illustration isolated on white background. By dariaustiugova

Bible quotes: New American Bible

Edited and formatted by Jenny Margotta, editorjennymargotta@mail.com

Book Cover Design: Michelle Prebble, Prime 9 Designs, prime9designs.com

Printed and published in the United States of America

10 9 8 7 6 5 4 3 2 1

For the Creator

"Praise the Lord, for He is good, for His mercy endures forever."

(Psalm 136:1)

Acknowledgments

The November and December holiday season fills me with joy, and I'm always grateful to spend time with family and friends. I find immense pleasure in watching holiday movies, savoring delicious meals over great conversations, and participating in many other fun and joyous celebrations of the season.

Christmas holds a special place in my heart. In writing *Once Upon a Cove Christmas*, I aimed to share a story that goes beyond the typical holiday narrative. It's a story that demonstrates how the season is not just about the festivities, gifts, or trimmings but rather a profound celebration of our Lord's birth and ultimate sacrifice—to pay our debt so that we may live. *"For God so loved the world that he gave his only Son so that everyone who believes in him might not perish but might have eternal life."* (John 3:16). Through the characters' actions and lives, I hope to convey how we might keep the Christmas spirit alive throughout each year.

As always, I would like to express my deepest gratitude to my parents, brothers, sister, their spouses and children, and all my extended family.

I'm also grateful for my many wonderful friends, whom I've mentioned in previous book dedications, and to give a special shout-out this time to my Magnificat sisters, Noreen Fortier, Louise Erickson, Jeanne Potter, Christina Silvas, Donna Ross, Elise Botch, and Monique Moussot, as well as Donna Ostrander, Nada Prskalo, and Teri Thompson. Your support and love are truly gifts.

May this Christmas and future holiday seasons bring you and all those you love abundant peace, love, joy, and blessings.

I invite you to visit my official website, where you can find information about my books, *Simply Delicious Living with Maryann*®

TV series, and online magazine. Discover easy, delicious recipes, cooking videos, and inspiration for joyful living.

Website & Simply Delicious Living with Maryann® Online Blog & Magazine:

https://www.MaryannRidiniSpencer.com

Amazon Author Page:

https://www.amazon.com/stores/Maryann-Ridini-Spencer%20/author/B06XBHH6YK

With love,

Maryann

The Greatest Gift

by Maryann Ridini Spencer

Hundreds of years before the Son of Man took human form,
The Good Book tells of a Savior yet to be born—*The Messiah*—
To a Virgin, and hailing from the line of David,
In the little town of Bethlehem—
A city not far from Jerusalem.

On that Holy pilgrimage,
Following a star so bright,
Three Wise Kings ventured out in the cold, wintry night,
To present their blessings, gifts, and praise,
To the King of Kings
Our Lord and Savior—
Fully Man and Fully Divine—
Who, by obedient act, will one day pay,
For the world's transgressions.
Oh, what a tragic yet glorious day.

Wrapped in swaddling clothes and set in a manger,
No room at the inn,
Lays The Prince of Peace,
God's precious Son—
The Sacrificial Lamb,
Born to save humankind,
So that God's flock might one day enter,
By following The Word,
To that place on High,
Where The Father's children will live, *never to die.*

Prologue

Lavender Hill Cove, New York – Present Day
Six weeks before Christmas

"T'was the night before Christmas, and all through the house, not a creature was stirring, not even a mouse," Ella Martin softly speaks as she reads to a class of adorable elementary school children at Lavender Hill Cove's historic library. The children, filled with excitement, listen intently and with wide-eyed wonder to the classic tale based on the poem "A Visit from St. Nicholas" by Clement Clarke Moore. Outside the library's cozy environment and large paned windows, snow flurries tumble from the overcast sky and gently caress the landscape.

The library, built in 1862 and once home to the Independent Congregational Church, was transformed into a library in the early nineteenth century. Today, the converted building, with its Italianate gable roof and Gothic-headed windows and doors, stands one-and-a-half stories and boasts a distinctly New England character. It houses a public library and many historical documents dating from Lavender Hill Cove's founding in the mid-1600s to the present day. It's a formidable example of "adaptive reuse" of a historic structure.

As Ella reads to the children, library staff place twenty-five little red velvet bags, each with a holiday book, a candy cane, and a tiny box of chocolates wrapped up with a bow by the library doors. The gift bags, a donation from Firefly Lane Farm Catering and Events, a company Ella co-owns with her childhood friend, Sophia Abrams, will be given to the children as a holiday treat upon leaving the session's reading.

"But I heard him exclaim, 'ere he drove out of sight, Happy Christmas to all, and to all, a good night!" Ella ends the story with dramatic emphasis.

"Ho, ho, ho!" yells Tommy Burke as the other children follow suit, some clapping, some shouting, "Merry Christmas!" with glee.

"This story is about Santa delivering gifts to those deserving on Christmas Eve. But does anyone know why Christmas is so important? It's not just the presents." Ella looks about the room at all the cherubic faces.

"Oh, oh!" squirms a five-year-old blonde with cascading curls, wearing a Christmas sweater, corduroy pants, and a nametag reading *Cindy*.

Ella points to Cindy, encouraging the little one who can barely contain her enthusiasm to answer.

"Jesus was born!"

"That's right, Jesus was born. The Word became flesh and lived among us," acknowledges Ella from John 1:14.

"I'm going to sing Happy Birthday to baby Jesus on Christmas," exclaims Cindy, followed by several other classmates who commit to doing the same.

"Now, children. Ms. Martin was very nice to drop by and read to us today. What do we say to Ms. Martin?" asks Doris Banks, the head librarian. Doris, dressed in a pretty holiday-red turtleneck and black skirt, with her gray hair in a fashionable French twist, looks to the young students to see who will raise their hand to answer. "Yes, Nadine." Doris nods, indicating for Nadine to answer.

"Thank you, Ms. Martin!" answers the sweet child. Other students exclaim the same sentiment enthusiastically.

"And what do we say to Ms. Martin about the holiday gift bags she brought for you?"

"Thank you, Ms. Martin!" roar the children. "We love you!"

"You are so very welcome." Ella chuckles. "Merry Christmas!" She bids the children goodbye from the library's door as they exit and pick up their gift bags. She feels as if her heart is about to burst. "They are precious."

"That they are," agrees Doris. "Thank you again for your time and generosity."

"I really enjoy being a part of the Children's Corner and reading to the little ones. I get such a kick from the things that come out of their mouths," Ella replies with another chuckle.

"Out of the mouths of babes. They tell it like it is. Ooh. Look!" Doris points toward the outside, where the snow is gathering into small drifts.

"I better get moving on home while the streets are still relatively clear." Ella grabs her coat and purse and makes a beeline for the door.

On her drive home, Ella marvels at the town's quiet beauty and festively decorated streets and shops. Victorian homes sparkle with holiday lights, and the warm glow from their kitchen and living room windows, along with twinkling stars in the night sky, illuminate the surrounding darkness.

A stabbing feeling suddenly pierces Ella's heart as she thinks of past Christmases with her late husband, Jack, who, in the prime of his life, was cut down in an airplane accident. She breathes deeply to anchor herself.

A few short years ago, we celebrated together . . . how life has changed.

After a severe glitch in their marriage led Ella to her childhood hometown of Lavender Hill Cove for some rest, familial support, and regrouping, Jack had a change of heart about his desire to divorce. However, fate had other plans. Flying from their home in California to meet Ella in New York to forge a new beginning in their marriage, Jack perished when the plane he was on crashed during a storm.

Still coming to terms with Jack's death, Ella entered into a new business endeavor, Firefly Lane Farm Catering and Events, with her lifelong friend Sophia Abrams. The business with Sophia, followed by purchasing and renovating her charming, New England-style beach house on a one-acre parcel with panoramic views of the Peconic Bay, has helped occupy Ella's thoughts and facilitate healing.

Whenever thinking of the past makes her feel sad, Ella reminds herself to be grateful for her friends, family, and home, and in doing so, her spirit lifts.

The beautiful landscape and historic homes, farms, and shops along Main Road, the central throughway in Lavender Hill Cove, create a magical scene akin to an image found in a tabletop picture book or a series of Thomas Kinkade paintings.

"Wow!" says Ella in awe as she passes one of the local vineyards decked out in a gorgeous array of sparkling white lights and an eye-catching nativity scene on its front lawn.

How gorgeous.

Moments later, a gust of howling wind suddenly rocks the car. Looking directly at the deserted country road ahead and then into the glimmering sky, Ella gasps. An unmistakable chill runs up her spine when, in the distant sky, a shooting star weaves across the darkened night.

Christmas magic. It's in the air!

Deck the Halls

"Blessed is the season which engages the whole world in a conspiracy of love."

~Hamilton Wright Mabie,
American essayist, editor, critic, and lecturer

Chapter One

The stars in the night sky form a glimmering blanket over the still waters of the Peconic Bay and continue to illuminate Ella's drive home.

After her busy but productive workday, she relishes the thought of unwinding at home over a tasty meal and a quiet evening doing whatever thrills her heart.

Dinner by the living room fireplace will be sublime.

Ella's phone rings and Sophia's name and number pops up on the car console. "Hey, Soph, what's up?"

"I forgot to mention that I have a bunch of personal appointments tomorrow, and I was wondering what you might think about working from home for the day."

"Works for me. I've got some holiday tasks to tend to and could use the time."

"Great. I'll be in touch. Text if you need to. Bye."

After the call with Sophia, Ella's mind drifts to her beach house, which closed escrow some two years ago. With its cedar shake exterior and large wrap-around porch, it had great bones, but it had been stuck in a 1970s-time warp and needed some serious TLC to remodel it to her taste.

Undaunted by the prospect of transforming the unpolished gem into a cozy country French farmhouse, not a day goes by when Ella doesn't thank the good Lord for the blessing of having been led to finding it. Nor does she neglect to say a prayer for the former owner, Mrs. Green, an elderly sweetheart who, after her husband's passing, realized it was time to move in with her daughter and accepted Ella's modest offer.

Mrs. Green had a tough time letting go of the family home, a place she had cherished for so long. It was the very foundation of her life, the place where she and her husband had started their journey as a couple, and where they had watched their children grow. Her main concern was finding a buyer who would appreciate and love her home as much as she did. When she met Ella, her heart rested because, intuitively, she knew that Ella would be such an owner.

Turning into the driveway toward her property's detached two-car garage, Ella glances at a local realtor's "For Sale" sign posted at the entrance of the driveway next door. Even though it's been several months since the Robinsons moved to Florida, she can't help but notice how lonely the house looks tonight—all dark with no signs of light, life, or Christmas spirit.

As she exits her car, Ella sends a silent prayer into the night. She hopes that her new neighbors will be as warm and friendly as the Robinsons and that the Robinsons will find the happiness they deserve in their new home.

Dinner is re-heated chicken tikka masala leftovers—a care package from a family meal at Ella's parents' house the previous evening with her siblings, Julie and Justin, Julie's husband, Tom, and Justin's girlfriend, Heather.

For dessert, Ella sinks into an oversized slipcovered loveseat in her home's great room to savor a cup of apple-cinnamon-spice tea by the roaring fire. Bathed, and cozy in her PJs and robe, Ella decides to skip the mindless TV surfing and, instead, turns on the local news.

"While Christmas may be in the air, several local retail stores are feeling there is a Scrooge in their midst." On television, an attractive male reporter walks past several store windows decorated for Christmas. He stops in front of a shop window where the holiday trimmings have been decimated.

"I just can't believe someone would destroy my holiday display," laments the shop owner on camera. "They tore down my lights, broke my Santa, and spray-painted my windows with black paint. Let me tell you, it's put a real damper on my holiday spirit." The shop owner's distress is palpable even through the TV screen.

How awful.

Ella continues to watch as the news story cuts to a police officer on the scene.

"It's a shame," remarks the officer. "These menacing attacks on local businesses and homes are a real nuisance, and we're investigating who the culprits might be. Please call the number on your screen with any tips." A local number scrolls across the bottom of the screen as the camera cuts to another newscaster.

Ella sighs with disgust. She clicks off the TV, trading her remote for her latest library read—a compilation of the best-loved Christmas stories and poems from literary masters Louisa May Alcott, Charles Dickens, Hans Christian Andersen, O. Henry, and others.

Now, these are the stories I want to fill my mind with before bed.

Ella devours O. Henry's "The Gift of the Magi" and other tales until another warm cup of soothing tea beckons. She heads toward the kitchen to turn on the kettle.

Her attention is piqued when the thrashing and howling wind outside becomes a barrage of piercing cries rattling her kitchen windowpanes. Curious, Ella peers out the window. The reflection of light from the stars in the night sky over the bay illuminates the Robinsons' porch next door, and Ella sees, or so she thinks, a white figure in silhouette floating across the Robinsons' veranda.

Impossible. The house is empty—not haunted.

The kettle's ear-piercing whistle snaps Ella out of her reverie. As she heads toward the stove to turn off the gas, she notices the time on the stove clock: 9:30 p.m.

And no realtor will be showing the house at this late hour.

Brushing off the ghostly vision, Ella picks a fresh teabag from a basket resting on a kitchen-nook-turned-coffee-and-tea bar and pours hot water into a large mug. Another look outside the window while the tea steeps confirms that all is well. This time, there is no movement.

Seconds later, Ella's phone beeps. Her sister, Julie, is responding to Ella's text earlier in the day.

Tom and I would love to come to dinner tomorrow night and help you decorate your tree. XO Julie.

Ella texts back.

Come around 4:00 pm to decorate. We'll have dinner at 6:00.

Ella smiles when Julie replies to Ella's comment with a heart emoji.

Picking up her tea mug, she returns to her reading chair. Several hours later, unable to keep her eyes open, she turns off the gas fireplace, deposits her teacup into the kitchen sink, and heads toward bed.

The next morning, even though Ella and Sophia agreed to work in their home offices for the day, Ella rises at 6 a.m., her body clock tuned to her weekday rising time.

Preferring to work professionally, even at home, Ella changes out of her PJs, showers, and dresses in comfortable slacks and a sweater. She takes her meal of avocado toast and coffee to her office computer, where she tends to her emails and some organizational needs for Firefly Lane Farm Catering and Events for the next several hours. Then, in preparation for the evening dinner with her sister and brother-in-law, she sets the dining room table with her favorite rose-patterned china.

Ella has always loved the classic pattern with its beautifully embossed roses in an elegant shade of pink, with green leaves and olive-green stems trimming the edge of each plate. She places each dish on an attractive, woven gold placemat. Next, at the nearby credenza, she opens the wood box that houses her sterling silver. A delicate rose design graces the silverware's edges, and the base perfectly complements the china.

Ella expertly arranges the silverware, water, and wine glasses in appropriate positions for each table setting. Then she places a folded gold napkin in a pretty pink rose napkin holder on top of each salad plate.

The dreamy centerpiece—an antique silver pitcher, a

consignment store find—is filled to overflowing with a bouquet of pink roses that Ella picked up at the local market a few days prior. To keep the flowers fresh and perky, she changes the water, adding several ice cubes.

In the kitchen, she removes a large glass container filled with tomato sauce, meatballs, and sausages from the freezer and places the dish in the fridge to defrost. Tonight's dinner will be easy-peasy. For starters, a leafy green salad with tomato, red onion, candied walnuts, and homemade parmesan croutons served with a tangy lemon vinaigrette dressing and crusty French bread followed by the spaghetti-and-meatball main course. It takes about thirty minutes to whip up an apple-spice crumble for dessert that will go great with a dab of vanilla bean ice cream—a tasty treat at the end of the meal.

After her kitchen duties, Ella drags a large cardboard box housing her prized, fake 7-foot balsam fir Christmas tree up from the basement. Another bargain, although this one was found online. The tree's three pieces easily fit together, making assembly a breeze. She covers the base with a fluffy white, snow-like skirt. Unraveling strings of lights, she slips the plug into the socket. With a decorator's touch, she drapes the white, sparkling lights over the tree limbs.

It's beginning to look a lot like Christmas!

Ella chuckles as she peeks at the wall clock. The fact that it's only noon means she'll have a good chunk of the afternoon to check out the sales at the local Christmas tree shop, one of her favorite places. She always finds joy in discovering unique tree ornaments that perfectly match her silver, white, gold and glass-themed decorated tree.

A Christmas Blessing

"Christmas waves a magic wand over this world, and behold,

everything is softer and more beautiful."

~Norman Vincent Peale,
American writer and minister

Chapter Two

Ella pulls her car onto the gravel driveway of Mimi's Christmas Tree Shop, a red country barn turned into a charming retail store, and parks near other vehicles. As soon as she enters the enchanting venue, the aromatic fragrance of cinnamon greets her. The perfume emanates from pinecones wrapped in mesh-casing sacks that fill the large wood barrel to the right of the entrance. Unable to resist this favorite holiday scent and anticipating the lovely aroma in her home, Ella tosses one of the sacks tied with a gold satin bow into a wire shopping basket.

Mimi's shop features all types of Christmas fare—faux trees of balsam fir, spruce, frosted alpine, evergreen, blue and white pine, and others in various shapes and sizes, as well as a plethora of tree ornaments, garlands, signs, plaques, candles, tableware, and baskets filled with holiday treats that create an unforgettable winter wonderland shopping experience.

A tall evergreen displays vintage-style ornaments that captivate Ella. She examines several beauties in gold, silver, and white, and eventually picks four glass-and-gold angel ornaments and three Victorian hearts adorned with gold brocade fabric and frilly lace ribbon with strategically placed pearls. As she continues to scan the store for other finds, Ella selects several hanging glass icicles that she knows will beautifully reflect the white lights on her tree. Next, she scoops up a miniature sleigh—a perfect display for the cinnamon-scented pinecones. At the checkout, the spicy scent of allspice and ginger emerges from a basket of homemade gingerbread men, each decoratively wrapped in transparent foil and tied up with a red bow.

Ella's eyes fixate on the cookies.

Yum!

"My wife made them this morning." Mr. James winks. "They're delicious."

"I bet. I'll take four," Ella says. She'll gift her sister and brother-in-law tonight and take two into work tomorrow morning so she and Sophia can have a yummy afternoon snack.

Ella hands Mr. James her credit card. While waiting to complete the sale, she notices a sign by the register announcing a nearby estate sale and grabs a flyer before leaving the store.

Not one to resist an intriguing antique store or estate sale, Ella programs her car's GPS to the address on the flyer. Traveling several miles down Main Road, she heeds a sign staked into the ground that reads "Estate Sale This Way" and turns onto a secluded, tree-lined street, at the end of which sits a well-maintained Victorian majestically perched on a bluff overlooking the bay.

Ella parks to the right of the stately home and approaches the "Enter" sign by the front door. Once inside, Ella takes note of the impressive foyer which boasts a luxurious marble floor and, to the right, a beautifully appointed spiral staircase that leads up to a second-floor, wrap-around landing. Ahead, voices emanate behind two expertly crafted mahogany doors where a sign reads, "Sale Entrance," and Ella proceeds down the imposing hallway.

Inside the splendid room, gleaming hardwood floors and high ceilings create an atmosphere of elegance. The walls are adorned with rich-looking cranberry- and pink-striped wallpaper, complemented by white crown molding. In this luxurious setting, a distinguished gray-haired man of about seventy-five, dressed in crisp charcoal gray pants, a matching turtleneck, and a tan cashmere sport coat, converses with a couple. Other men and women mull about the room and scrutinize items for sale.

Ella gravitates to an antique jewelry display. Next, unique pieces of furniture and fine art intrigue her. She notices a stunning oil resembling one of the old, historic, iconic barns in the area. The painting is a steal for seventy dollars and would make a great Christmas present for Sophia.

Amid all the mesmerizing items stands a stunning porcelain figurine of the Holy Family: St. Joseph with the Blessed Virgin Mary holding a baby Jesus. This exquisite piece measures approximately twelve inches in height. Joseph and Mary stand on a glittering cotton and mica bed made to resemble a cloud. St. Joseph, with a gold halo, wears robes of brown and green. Mary wears an ivory-colored silk dress and a sky-blue coat covered with sparking stars, lace, and gold trim at the edges. A glittering gold crown with twelve points sits on her head, and her luscious mane of brown curls reaches beyond Our Lady's shoulders. Mary's hand-painted porcelain face is lovely, serene, and regal. She holds a smiling Jesus wrapped in a white blanket and wearing a gold crown. Behind the Holy Family is gold and blue roping tinsel with blue, gold, and silver glass garland beads shaped to look like the stained-glass window of a church. The sale tag is marked $250. Ella is smitten.

Absolutely stunning.

"Hello, Miss, may I help you?" asks the distinguished-looking gentleman in the cashmere sports coat.

"This statue is gorgeous," starts Ella.

"Not just a statue, although you could use it as one. But take a look," says the man, turning the item over and showing Ella a cone shape. "The Holy Family is a vintage tree-topper."

"Oh," coos Ella. "It would look beautiful on my tree, which is bare right now. My name's Ella, by the way."

"Lester Sinclair. Nice to meet you, Ella." Lester extends his hand to shake hers. "Do you live in Lavender Hill Cove or are you just visiting?"

"Born and raised here. I moved to California for a time but moved back two years ago."

"Happy to be home?"

"I love it here."

"What type of work do you do?"

"I'm a partner in the newly formed Firefly Lane Farm Catering and Events."

"Oh, I know Firefly Lane Farm. My wife, Penelope, and I often purchase organic produce at their farm stand. I didn't know they do events."

"My business partner, Sophia Abrams, and I are putting together an event—we're calling it "Once Upon a Cove Christmas Gala"—to raise funds to add a children's reading and learning extension onto the Lavender Hill Cove Library. Shall I send you an invite?"

"Absolutely. I love the title. It's perfect since the gala is raising funds for the library. I'll get you my card." Lester walks to a desk to retrieve a silver holder. "Here you go." Lester and Ella exchange cards.

"How much is the oil of the old barn?" Ella points to the framed canvas. "It would make a great Christmas present for my friend."

"Seventy dollars. If you purchase it, I'll gift you the vintage topper."

"What?" Ella's mouth drops open.

"You seem to love it, and it needs a good home. Besides, it's Christmas."

"That is so generous, so kind." Ella hands Lester her credit card. "Are you absolutely sure?"

"It's the holidays; it feels good to do good and make another person smile." Lester returns the credit card and hands Ella her receipt. He carefully wraps the oil painting in paper then bubble wrap and places it in a large bag. "I'll let you in on a little secret," he says. Ella's eyes widen, and her ears perk up. "A family friend, a priest, blessed this tree topper years ago. So, as a sacramental, sacred, and holy, it's set apart from other objects."

"Are you sure you want to part with it?"

"My wife and I decorate for the holidays, but we usually celebrate at our children's homes, so we rarely put up a big tree. It's a shame to leave this beautiful piece inside a box in our hall closet. Besides, it's time to pay it forward. I have a gut feeling you'll appreciate the ornament and will give it a good home."

"I will."

Lester hands Ella the paper bag with her purchases. "Penelope and I will look forward to getting the invite to your fundraiser."

Ella nods. "Thank you. Merry Christmas."

"Merry Christmas."

"The tree topper is quite a stunner," agrees Ella's sister, Julie, later that evening as Julie and her husband, Tom, help Ella decorate her tree following their spaghetti-and-meatball dinner. A roaring gas-log fire in the fireplace and the harmonious Christmas instrumentals that play on a PBS television special add to the cozy atmosphere. Outside, a gentle snow falls on the landscape.

"I love that it's been blessed and now a sacramental which disposes people to receive God's grace and love," comments Ella.

"We all need as much of that as we can get." Tom chuckles securing the vintage topper in its rightful place. "Maybe I should start handing out some blessed items to my clients." Tom is one of Long Island's top criminal defense attorneys.

"Your clients could use it," replies Julie to her husband. "They especially need God's mercy."

"Ouch." Tom chuckles again.

"Say, Ella, how are you coming on your Christmas shopping?" asks Julie.

"I still have a few more items to get."

"I haven't even started. If you can, want to come shopping with me tomorrow?"

"Sure." Ella puts the last ornaments on the tree. "Hey, guys, it's really snowing now," she says in a happy, sing-song voice as she glances out the living room window.

"The afternoon newscast said to expect at least four inches," reports Tom.

"Four I can handle," pipes up Julie. "But I'm not ready for a heavy storm yet. I'm hoping this year will be like last year—mild."

"I hear you, Sis. Now that the tree's decorated, how about some apple-spice crumble and coffee?"

"And maybe a cappuccino?" asks Tom like a little boy. "I love the way you make it."

Ella nods. "A cappuccino can definitely be arranged."

Later, as Ella, Julie, and Tom are gathered around the dining table enjoying dessert, a TV news report interrupts the holiday music and cuts to the vandalism of holiday displays in Lavender Hill Cove.

"There have been a lot of pesky things happening around town lately." Julie jumps out of her chair to turn up the TV volume.

"Those darn kids threw rocks wrapped in snow and broke all the front store windows," laments an unhappy man in his sixties. "If I had my way, those hoodlums would be locked up."

"How many kids participated?" asks the young, attractive female reporter.

"About six."

"Well, there you have it," says the reporter to the camera. "This is just one of several recent crimes involving a gang of teenagers. If you or anyone you know sees a crime, please call the Lavender Hill Cove Police Department." A telephone number flashes across the bottom of the screen as Julie lowers the TV volume.

"How horrible—and mean-spirited," comments Ella. "I watched a news story about another trashing of holiday displays last night. Julie, what have you heard about it?" Ella knows that Julie, a detective with the Lavender Hill Cove police, will have the inside scoop.

"Kids have been breaking store windows, destroying holiday lights and ornaments, stealing retail goods, and there have even been some home break-ins."

"How do you know it's just kids?"

"Shop owners and residents see a group of rowdy kids running away from the crime scenes."

"Are you talking about a local gang?"

"Could be."

"In Lavender Hill Cove?"

"Hey, no town is immune. We're investigating."

Ella shakes her head, sad to hear about the current reality. "On a lighter note, more dessert, anyone?"

"Since you insist." Tom grins and holds out his plate.

"Honestly, Tom, sweetie, where do you put it?" questions Julie.

"I work up an appetite being in court all day."

"Why can you eat whatever you want, and I have to calorie count?" Julie sighs and takes a sip of her coffee.

"Just lucky, I guess."

When Julie leans over to give Tom a peck, they lock lips for a few seconds.

The love shared between her sister and brother-in-law at one of the most joyous times of the year suddenly reminds Ella of Jack and all that she's lost with Jack's death. She feels a pain stab her heart and quickly recites a silent prayer that has become her mantra when feeling the overwhelming loss of Jack.

Father, I trust in You and Your will for my life. Calm my heart and protect me from fear and anxiety. Surround me with Your peace, as only You can comfort me.

Later that evening, alone in her bedroom, Ella opens a large antique white chest and removes a sizeable green album packed with images from past Christmases. She carries it to her bedroom loveseat, turns on the floor lamp, sits, and peruses the photos. Memories stir. Ella habitually keeps almost every holiday greeting card, a tradition that has created a beautiful continuity in her life, chronicling her and her siblings in various poses each year until they graduated high school. There's an adorable image of Ella and her siblings, Julie and Justin, sitting on Santa's lap at the local department store, and others, showing the three of them, ecstatic as they open Santa's gifts on Christmas mornings. As she turns the pages, Ella smiles at photos of her maternal and paternal grandparents, aunts, uncles, and cousins gathered around various holiday dining tables. She has even kept a few photos taken with her high school and college boyfriends at various holiday celebrations. Turning to images from more recent years, Ella lands on a photo of her and Jack celebrating their first Christmas. And there are other Christmases there too.

"Oh, Jack," Ella murmurs sorrowfully. "I miss you."

Look at how cute we were. You were so handsome...we were so happy then.

Ella starts to tear up, remembering. After a time, unwilling to stir any more memories, she closes the album. Her tears flow readily now, and as they do, she returns the album to its storage place and then heads to the master bath in search of a tissue.

At her bedside, she places the tissue box on the nightstand, turns out the light, and slips between the covers. Despite trying to shut her mind off, she continues to think about Jack and all the happy holidays shared. As she does, the tears come and go and sometimes her tears turn into laughter as she remembers funny moments—until reality hits again—*Jack is gone*— and she sobs until her tears run out.

In the Eye of the Storm

"In all circumstances, hold faith as a shield,
To quench all the flaming arrows of the evil one."

(Ephesians 6:16)

Chapter Three

"What do you think about this blouse for Mom?" Julie holds up a pretty, dark-pink, button-down silk blouse for Ella to examine during their holiday shopping spree the following day.

"Love it. Mom loves pink, and it'll go great with the rose print silk scarf I got for her."

"Perfect." Julie places the blouse in her shopping cart. "Now, on to the men's department."

"My Amex is smoking." Julie laughs as she and Ella climb into Julie's SUV after several hours of shopping. Famished, the sisters decide on lunch at The Cove, a quaint little café in the heart of Lavender Hill Cove's Old Town, before Ella heads back to her office to tend to a few details before calling it quits for the weekend.

At 2:00, the café is bursting with patrons. The fragrant aromas of fresh coffee brewing and various baked goods in the oven make Ella's stomach growl.

A young hostess leads the sisters to a window table and lays down two menus. "Can I get you anything to drink?"

"Unsweetened iced tea for me," announces Ella.

"Ditto," replies Julie.

"This place smells great. I'll have the veggie frittata," remarks Ella. "I love how they serve it with a side of fresh greens, goat cheese crumbles, and candied pecans."

"Sounds divine, but I had eggs for breakfast, and since I worked up a sweat shopping, I think I'm going to go for the café brie burger—lettuce wrapped—with sweet potato fries." Always alert to any calls, Julie pulls her cell out of her purse and places it on the restaurant table.

As they sip their teas after placing their lunch orders, the sisters hear a series of rumbling sounds and turn to see what's happening. Two teenage boys wearing black hoodies and dark-colored scarves pulled up above their noses, which hide their faces, are seen aggressively pushing past several patrons as they exit the restaurant.

"They took our purses!" screams a classy, gray-haired woman in a green dress as she stands up from her lunch table.

"Help!" cries the woman's lunch companion with a short platinum bob.

"Oh, my goodness, that woman in the green dress is Doris Banks from the library where I read to the kids," gasps Ella in horror.

Julie jumps to attention and races out the café's front door. Ella follows while the other patrons look on, shocked.

Moments later, Julie, on her cell phone and fired up, walks back into the café with Ella. The sisters join Doris and her companion, who are deep in conversation with the restaurant manager.

"I called the incident into the police department," Julie says. "My name is Officer Julie Landon with the Lavender Hill Cove Police Department, but I'm off duty. One of my colleagues will be here shortly to complete a report. I'm so sorry. I know the boys' faces were covered, but did you happen to see anything that could identify them?

"The only thing I saw was one of the boys had a skull and cross bones tattooed onto the back side of his hand. I'm Louise Goodson, by the way," the woman with the platinum bob says.

"Doris, are you okay?" asks Ella as Doris clutches her chest. "Is your heart hurting? Do you need an ambulance?"

"No, no, Ella, I'm okay." Doris shakes her head. "Clutching my chest is just a habit I have when I'm anxious or upset."

"How will we pay for our lunch?" laments Louise.

"I can call my husband, Larry," replies Doris. "He'll take care of the bill."

"Don't worry, lunch is on the café today," ensures the restaurant manager, a middle-aged with a name tag that reads "Rita Singer. "Thank you, Officer for your help."

Julie smiles and shakes Rita's hand.

"Doris, Louise, this is my sister, Julie," Ella shares.

"Thank you, Officer Landon," replies Louise.

"We appreciate your efforts," adds Doris.

In less than five minutes, two uniformed policemen show up. Once the officers speak briefly to Julie, they lead Doris and Louise toward the manager's office to give their statements.

Despite the upsetting circumstances and heavy atmosphere, Julie and Ella sit back down to try to eat their lunch but to no avail.

"I think I lost my appetite," remarks Ella.

"Me too," Julie says, stirring ketchup on her plate with a fry.

"Let's take it to go. We're near my house; we can relax and eat there."

Julie nods in agreement.

At the register, Julie and Ella attempt to pay for lunch.

"My manager, Rita, said your lunch is comped, too," the cashier says, refusing their money.

"Can we thank her?" asks Ella.

"She's in the back room talking to the police."

"Well, please tell her we said thank you," comments Julie.

Ella acknowledges the act of kindness with a smile. "Whew, that was intense," she notes on the drive back to her place.

"Yeah. I hope the police catch those boys. They looked young."

"I wonder what their story is."

Julie shrugs. "Hey, Sis, my gas tank is on empty." Julie pulls her SUV into a nearby gas station and starts to fill up. A few seconds later, a charcoal gray Ford Ranger pulls up to an adjacent pump.

Ella looks through the SUV's passenger window. The logo on the side of the truck reads "Grant & Sons." Moments later, Harrison Grant, a tall, dark-haired man wearing jeans, sneakers, and a classic, navy-colored, hooded, down-filled parka emerges from the truck. He sees Ella almost immediately and waves. Ella rolls down her window.

"Hey, how are you?" Harrison walks over to Ella's window. His friendly blue eyes sparkle.

"It's been quite an afternoon."

"Oh?"

Ella relays the details of the lunch-time crime, and after finishing gassing up the SUV, Julie adds her two cents.

"How's your house doing these days?" asks Harrison after expressing dismay about recent local crimes.

Ella originally met Harrison when his company remodeled Firefly Lane Farm's barn and outdoor pavilion. Impressed at his craftmanship, Ella asked Harrison to build a pergola on her home's back patio when the Firefly Lane job was complete.

"Looking good. I've been loving it, even in winter. I've put a few space heaters on the deck to keep me warm out there. I'm planning a few more projects, so I'll let you know when I need your services again."

"Well, we don't have to wait that long. Would you like to grab a coffee sometime?"

"I, um, I—" stutters Ella, surprised by the offer.

After Harrison and his brother, Luke, built Ella's pergola, the brothers took Ella and Sophia out for an impromptu concert and dinner in the park. However, that was months ago. While Ella and Harrison had chemistry, life got hectic and took them in different directions.

"I'd like that," replies Ella with a sultry smile once she's composed.

"Great. I have your number. I'll give you a ring tonight. Maybe we can set something for later in the week." When Ella nods in agreement, Harrison waves goodbye and walks back toward the gas pumps as Ella powers up her window.

Julie starts to whistle as she pulls out of the station onto the main road. "A coffee date, huh?"

"He's nice and very accomplished," states Ella matter-of-factly, ignoring Julie's jesting.

Julie chuckles. "Excellent eye candy, too."

"Agreed."

"Well, you'll have to give me a play-by-play afterward."

"If there's something to share, you'll be the first to know."

"Say, Sis, I need to drop by the station. Do you mind?" Julie asks. "I left my gym bag in my office, and I need it."

"Sure. I have to make a pit stop anyway."

A few minutes later, Julie pulls into the Lavender Hill Cove Police station, a one-story, traditional Colonial red brick building with a dormer roof and two white pillars flanking the three steps leading up to the front entrance.

Ella follows Julie into the precinct and heads directly to the ladies' room while Julie goes to her office. When Ella returns to fetch Julie, she finds a distraught shop owner, Mr. Anderson, giving Julie's colleague an earful.

"Last month, hoodlums stole from my shop. Three weeks ago, it was a snowball with a stone through my glass window. Yesterday, the holiday tree and lights I had outside my store were destroyed! What good does filling out a report do? I want something done about this."

"Come with me, Mr. Anderson. Let's see what we can do," says Officer Tim Riley leading the irate business owner down the hall toward his office.

"See you later, Tim." Julie waves goodbye, feeling a stab of guilt that she's happy it's Tim dealing with Mr. Anderson and not her. Ella, silent, follows her sister to the car.

"Tim sure is in the line of fire," Ella says as she slides into the passenger seat.

"Yeah. I can't say that I blame Mr. Anderson, though."

"Do you think it's the same group of boys causing all this havoc?"

"Very probable. I'm sure there'll be a staff meeting on all the new developments. I feel everyone's pain, but I'll deal with it on duty. Tonight, I'm a free agent. Tom's working late. Want to bug Sophia and see what she's up to for dinner later? We could paint the town red."

"Sounds like a plan."

Three Hearts

"Relying on God has to begin all over again every day as if nothing had yet been done."

~~C.S. Lewis

Chapter Four

"Are you sure you're okay with dining at the Sandpiper?" asks Sophia, referring to Lavender Hill Cove's most popular restaurant and bar. She, Ella, and Julie drive toward the restaurant in Sophia's blue Ford Explorer. "When I called to make a reservation, they said Carter was out of town, and the Wine Country Ramblers are playing tonight."

"I'd be okay even if Carter was playing," says Ella about Carter Huxley, her on-again-off-again high school-crush-turned-international pop-and-country-music star and as it also happens, a Sandpiper partner.

Sophia shoots Ella a look of surprise.

"Yes, I was upset when he couldn't even refer to me as his girlfriend after months of dating."

"And backed out of everything he promised," pipes up Julie.

"Yeah, but I got over it."

After a chance meeting with Carter months after Jack's passing, for a brief moment in time, Ella and Carter reignited their romance until Ella discovered that Carter, like in high school, while monopolizing her time, heart, and attention with future promises of togetherness, was still not willing to commit to any one woman despite what he professed to Ella.

"Men are so spoiled these days," blurts out Julie angrily. "I'm sad to say, all women have had a hand in it. Giving too much too soon before a man truly commits." While Ella is accepting rejection gracefully, Julie is angry that Carter lured her sister in with sweet words and, in Julie's opinion, took advantage. After all, Ella is indeed a genuine catch, and after the death of her husband, she certainly didn't need that head- or heartache.

"I didn't give too much too soon," states Ella in her defense. "At least I was wise to that. If I had, I would be a wreck. Luckily, I followed the biblical teachings, and while waiting, I discovered the truth. Even though I wanted a different outcome, I didn't try to wear rose-colored glasses. And I'll tell you something else: I won't give *my all* until I have a ring on this finger." Ella points to the ring finger on her left hand.

"The sixties and seventies were good in many ways and bad in others. It turned out that the sexual revolution didn't help the women's cause for commitment, and it's only getting worse in this digital age." Sophia sighs. "So I agree and support you, girlfriend."

"Thanks." Ella, in the passenger seat, turns and smiles at Sophia.

"I'm glad Tom and I met when we were babies, so we never entered the dating scene," exclaims Julie. "I don't envy you gals dating today. It's a jungle out there."

Not a fan of valet parking, Sophia maneuvers her SUV into the Sandpiper's gravel parking lot, relieved to secure one of the few remaining parking spaces.

The ladies step onto the restaurant's welcoming, sizeable wrap-around porch. Two faux Christmas trees with sparkling white lights grace each side of the New England Colonial farmhouse's double-door entrance.

A pretty hostess in an attractive red silk top, black pants, and heels checks Sophia's name on the reservation log. "Do you prefer inside or out? We have space heaters on the patio."

Sophia looks at Ella and Julie.

"Inside," the sisters exclaim in unison, preferring a cozy, warm table inside versus risking a possible December chill.

"If you have a window table, that would be great," adds Ella.

"Follow me," says the hostess. She leads the ladies to a table with a beautiful view of Peconic Bay as the mesmerizing sky turns stunning shades of purply pink, orange, and yellow.

The ladies split a carafe of chardonnay and a large Caesar salad to start and order the Sandpiper specials—citrus salmon over a bed of potatoes au gratin with roasted winter vegetables for Julie and macadamia nut-encrusted halibut with Thai peanut sauce over Jasmine rice for Sophia and Ella.

"Oh, I meant to tell you, Lavender Hill Cove Travel will be donating a holiday package for the gala's silent auction," shares Sophia.

"Fantastic!" gushes Ella. "You know, with the recent local vandalism and thefts—*which is definitely not in line with the Christmas spirit*—maybe we can involve the local TV and radio stations to do a promotion."

"What type of promotion?"

"One to elicit community support for the retailers impacted by the vandalism."

"I like that idea," says Sophia as she munches on a bread stick.

"Maybe, while we collect silent auction items to raise funds for the library's new children's wing, we can also coordinate donors to contribute auction items to support the retailers."

"I like it," states Sophia. "That way, the entire community can be involved, which builds goodwill, support, and underscores the meaning of the season."

"We have several officers on the force who are members of the Knights of Columbus. I can hit them up if you'd like." Julie's offer meets with enthusiasm from Ella and Sophia.

"Cheers," says Ella as she, Julie, and Sophia hold up their wine glasses in a toast.

After dinner, the women make their way into the Sandpiper's lounge. Patrons sit at small round tables in the darkened room as the Wine Country Ramblers play. A few couples dance in front of the stage. Several songs later, the lead singer, Tex Bridges, introduces a well-known, special guest: Carter Huxley.

"I thought you said Carter was out of town," whispers Julie, leaning in to hear Sophia's answer.

"That's what the reservations attendant told me." Sophia shrugs innocently. Ella pretends not to be affected one way or another. However, as soon as Carter walks onto the stage, his handsome face, chiseled physique, and head of curly, sandy locks, combined with a natural charisma and sexy swagger, causes Ella's heart to leap. The audience erupts into thunderous applause and even a few catcalls. Trying to ignore her heightened senses, Ella takes a sip of her chardonnay to calm her nerves.

Knowing how fond her sister is of Carter, and afraid Ella might feel awkward seeing him, Julie gently squeezes Ella's arm as if to say, "It'll be okay."

Tex and Carter sing a few of Carter's well-known hits together, and to finish the music set, Carter sings his most recent multiplatinum recording, "Happy in the Heart of Home," after which he returns the stage to Tex and the Wine Country Ramblers.

"Ella!" Carter notices Ella and heads toward her table.

Ella takes a deep breath as she focuses on Carter's gorgeous, deep-set hazel eyes that would make any woman, at any age, swoon. "Hi," she replies keeping her cool.

"Would you mind if I join you all for a bit?" Carter acknowledges each of the ladies. Julie, still harboring resentment toward Carter because of his previous callous treatment of Ella, takes a sip of her drink to avoid greeting him. Sophia politely nods.

Only Ella responds. "Sure."

"Ladies, would you like anything?" Carter asks and motions to a pretty waitress passing by.

"Cappuccino." Julie finds her voice. "With a splash of rum."

"I'll second that," follows Sophia.

"Me, three," says Ella.

"And I'll take our Sandpiper Beer. Please bring a charcuterie dessert board, too. Thank you." Carter turns away from the waitress and back toward the women and asks, "When did you ladies arrive?"

"We had seven o'clock dinner reservations but stayed to hear the band," answers Sophia.

After several more minutes of conversation, Carter stands. "Ladies, it was wonderful talking, and I'd love to stay longer, but I've got some business with our house manager and chef now. Please stay as long as you like and order anything on the menu; it's on the house."

Moments later, the head hostess comes to the table and hands each lady a black leather check presenter housing their individual dinner credit card receipts. "The charges on your cards have been refunded. Dinner and the bar menu are on the house courtesy of Mr. Huxley. He insisted."

"Thank you," gushes Sophia as the head hostess returns to her post. "That was nice of him."

"Yes, it was," agrees Ella. "Very."

"Maybe we should order a private-selection bottle of wine from the vintage wine list." Julie scans the wine menu "Vintage selections *only* range from a thousand dollars on up," she says deadpan.

Sophia chuckles. "Gee, Julie, I never want to get on your bad side."

Ella laughs at the banter as she opens the black leather check presenter. Carter has written on her receipt: *I would love to talk more. I'll call you. –Carter.* She knows it's better to keep this news to herself— at least for now.

"What? You think I'm kidding about the wine?" Julie says sarcastically. "He said we can order anything."

"Julie! Come on, you must admit Carter was very hospitable tonight. Besides, I told you before, the circumstances surrounding our break stung, but we're friendly now."

"You're too nice, Ella. He treated you poorly, tied you up for months, and when it came down to it, he couldn't even refer to you as his girlfriend. He was sly and just said what a woman would want to hear. Oh, don't get me started."

"I know, Sis. He's got issues."

"Yeah, well, I should have ordered the steak and lobster for dinner," scoffs Julie.

"I love you, Sis," laughs Ella.

Later that evening, Ella sinks into the plush, slipcovered loveseat by her great room's hearth. The soft glow of the fire and the twinkling lights on her tree create a serene atmosphere. Sipping on her lemon-ginger tea, she finds herself enveloped in a cocoon of comfort and allows her thoughts to drift to her romantic life.

Jack was her love for over twenty years. His passing, now almost two years ago, still casts a shadow over Ella's daily life. There isn't a day that goes by when she doesn't miss him or think of him with a pang of sadness in her heart. The pain of his death was initially so unbearable that even the simplest tasks became a struggle. It was only through her work with Sophia on their startup Firefly Lane Farm Catering and Events that she found a way to move forward.

Finding purpose and taking one day at a time has been crucial to her healing. Learning to appreciate and relish the little things each day—like a soothing cup of tea, cozying up to a good book, tending to her herb garden, and sharing a relaxing meal with family and friends—has acted like a salve on an open wound. Ella has also found immense pleasure and comfort in remodeling and decorating her unique haven. Antique and estate sale hunting has been excellent medicine, taking her mind off her pain and focusing her creative energies on building a cozy nest for herself.

However, constant prayer—morning, noon, and night—has been the top healing remedy. Right after Jack's death, Ella would spend hours praying, saying the Rosary and asking Mother Mary and Jesus for help so that she might gain peace in her heart.

In church, the pastors talk about how every human being, at one time or another, suffers, and that, although we try to avoid it, suffering is an inevitable part of life on this earth following the fall of Adam and Eve. However, in suffering, uniting one's pain with Jesus's Passion, this redirection takes on *redemptive power* that a soul may offer up for oneself, others, or the salvation of souls.

Ella truly believes that Jesus walks with her, especially during tumultuous times, and when someone offers up their suffering, it's a powerful means by which people learn to love others like Christ. Thus, redemptive suffering can become, in fact, a form of healing and it has for Ella. Through her daily prayers, she has found immense peace and, even in her most profound loss, the comforting revelation that she is never alone.

Months after Jack's death, Ella was happy to reconnect with Carter. However, his pursuit of her and his words of commitment fell short. Although Ella proceeded with precaution to ascertain if Carter's interest was due to genuine affection with the possibility of a future together, once she became aware that they were actually on different pages, despite Carter's professions of love and a desire to spend a lifetime with her, a lightbulb went off in her head.

Carter wanted to be with me, lock me into a seemingly exclusive dating commitment, yet remain a free agent.

While tremendously disappointed, Ella, no stranger to heartache, had no choice but to stand up for what she knew was respectful and suitable for herself. It was hard to say no to Carter, but she knew she risked even more heartache if she didn't. When it came to a man saying he wasn't "all in," Ella believed the words of one of her favorite Bible verses: *"Behold, I am sending you out as sheep in the midst of wolves, so be wise as serpents and innocent as doves."* (Matthew 10:16)

Seconds later, a text pings Ella's phone. It's Carter.

> Great to see you tonight. I'm headed out of town for a recording session next week, but I will call you when I return. I'd love to take you to dinner. – Carter

Ella ponders Carter's offer and replies:

> Thank you for your hospitality in treating us to dinner tonight. We had a good time. Feel free to get in touch with me when you return. –Ella

While Ella feels excited receiving Carter's text, she is committed to not having any expectations or unrealistic fantasies. She wants to find out where Carter's head is at. Done with her evening novel reading and already washed and in her PJs, Ella turns off the living room light and heads for bed with her cell phone. Another text pings no sooner than she places her phone in its charger.

Hi, Ella. It was great to see you at the gas station today. I mentioned I would contact you later, so . . . Hello. I'd love to take you to coffee. How about lunch this week? Maybe Monday? Let me know what works for you.

–Harrison 😊

Ella chuckles at the smiley face. *Cute.* She heads to her home office to check her datebook, still preferring a calendar she can hold in her hand vs. the one on her phone—a bit old school, but it works for her.

"Let's see." She speaks out loud as she scans her datebook, noting that she has meetings on Wednesday and Friday. Monday for lunch will work. She heads back to her phone in the master bedroom and texts Harrison:

Hi, Harrison. Lunch on Monday works. What time and where?"

Harrison responds:

How about I come by your office around noon? I'd like to try The Cottage Dining and Reading Room. I hear they have great food and a nice ambiance. Okay?

Ella texts back.

I've been wanting to try that venue! See you Monday at noon. Sweet dreams. —Ella.

Having heard only good things about the new dining spot, Ella is thrilled Harrison is taking her to a venue she wants to sample. With two men seemingly in pursuit, she rethinks turning in and weighs reading vs. a mindless movie. While she is tempted to call Sophia and Julie to fill them in on her upcoming lunch with Harrison, knowing Sophia and Julie turn in early, the 11:30 p.m. time dissuades her. So, a mindless movie it is.

The Open Door

"Seek and you will find; knock and the door will be opened to you. For everyone who asks, receives; and the one who seeks, finds; and to the one who knocks, the door will be opened."

(Matthew 7:7-8)

Chapter Five

Ella chooses to sleep in the following morning. After a leisurely breakfast, she checks her emails and texts and then readies herself for Sunday mass at noon.

Arriving at the church a few minutes early, Ella engages in warm conversations with familiar faces in the vestibule. She then selects a pew near the altar. Happy to learn that Father Paul will deliver mass, as his sermons are always wonderfully inspiring, Ella sings the opening hymn with the other churchgoers.

After the Bible readings, Father Paul's homily delves into how, at The Last Supper, Our Lord knew his end was near and shared the meaning behind Jesus's washing of his disciples' feet.

Ella ponders Jesus' words, explaining that men become great by serving one another and not using authority over one another. She finds special meaning in the new commandment Jesus gave to his followers at the meal: "Love one another. As I have loved you, so you also should love one another." (John 13:34)

Lavender Hill Cove could learn from this teaching, thinks Ella, her mind reviewing all the recent vandalism causing so much distress.

"It was such a thought-provoking talk," Ella says. She is on her cell phone talking to Julie as she drives into town to pick up dessert for the family Sunday dinner. "It makes me feel like Sophia and I are on the right path with our gala. Father's Paul's homily was a type of confirmation—the importance of gathering the community to support one another and to treat each other with kindness, love, and respect—how all of us want to be treated."

"I'm proud of you, Sis," Julie states. "I'm really looking forward to the gala myself. Do you think you and Sophia will make it an annual event?"

"From your mouth to God's ears," Ella says as she pulls into the Love Street Bakery parking lot. "I'm at the bakery. I'll see you soon."

"What are you picking up?"

"It's a surprise."

"Torture my anticipating taste buds, go ahead. I won't hold it against you." Julie chuckles.

Normally, Ella would bake or prepare a dish to take to her parents' home for the family Sunday dinner. However, the week got away from her, and knowing how much her family loves this treat, Ella gets a kick out of how pleased and excited they'll be when they discover what's for dessert.

Ever since Ella can remember, her immediate family and, sometimes uncles, aunts, and cousins, have gathered on Sunday afternoons for a family meal. In later years, even while the extended family had other obligations, with children growing up, marrying, and having their own children, Ella's family maintained this well-loved tradition as much as possible.

"Hey, Dad!" Ella calls out as she enters her parents' front door.

Ella's father, Michael, sits on the great room sofa and looks up from his Sunday paper. His eyes light up when he sees his daughter. "Hello, sweetheart."

Ella bends down to give her father a peck on the cheek.

"Is that Ella?" Audrey, Ella's mother, calls out as Ella rounds the corner to the kitchen.

"Yup, it's me, Mom."

Audrey stops stirring the pot of tomato sauce on the stove to embrace her daughter. "How lovely you look, dear."

"Thanks, Mom. I got dressed to go to noon mass and came here right after.

"Your father and I went to the five o'clock last night."

"What time is everyone coming over?"

"The usual. I told Julie and Justin two o'clock for appetizers before dinner. What's in the pastry box?"

"Lemon-ricotta pie," sings Ella.

Audrey grins. "Oooh, yum. I planned on making a galette, so you saved me some work.

"What can I do to help?"

"Well, I breaded and baked the chicken. The sauce will be ready in a few. You can assemble the chicken parmesan and help me make a salad. We can store it in the fridge to dress later."

After washing her hands, Ella nods and retrieves the salad fixings from the fridge—mixed lettuce, mushrooms, Roma tomatoes, red onion, and black olives and begins to assemble the salad.

Whenever Ella visits her parents, perfect peace envelops her; she loves spending time with them. In their mid-seventies, they are still happy and fit, a living testament to love. They continue to complement each other perfectly, providing a powerful example of what a marriage should be—loving, devoted and committed to each other and their children. Her parents' love for one another, still strong after the decades, warms the heart.

"So, how goes it?" Audrey asks as she stirs the sauce.

"All's well with work. Sophia and I are figuring out the details for the holiday fundraiser. We must get it organized ASAP, but we can do it. We're used to working under pressure."

"I didn't mean work, honey. I mean, you, emotionally. I sense some sadness. Am I right?"

Ella nods. "You're always right."

"Tell me."

"It's the holidays . . . and I'm thinking of Jack."

"Oh, sweetheart." Audrey stops what she's doing, and she and Ella embrace. "Holidays are the hardest times when we're missing loved ones."

"Mom, do you think you can ever get over it when a loved one like a spouse dies?" Ella starts to tear up.

"There are so many stages of grief, and grief comes in waves. Sometimes, a place, thing, or person—can trigger a memory. It's not easy. But can a person ever get over the passing of a mate? Probably not entirely, because love lives on. However, I believe, with time, the burden can be lightened, especially with prayer and loving friends and family. And with healing, a woman as young as yourself, with so much love to give, well, if you keep yourself open, I believe you can find deep, lasting love again."

"Thank you, Mom."

"Would you like a cup of tea, dear?" asks Audrey, still holding Ella.

"How about a glass of . . . what is that liqueur I like at the holidays?"

"Grand Marnier?"

"That's it."

"Coming up." Audrey pulls a glass out of the kitchen cabinet and heads toward the liquor cabinet.

"Feel better," asks Audrey after Ella has had a few sips. "I can also sneak a brownie from our stash."

"Oh, bring it on. More sugar, especially chocolate, is one of nature's best medicines." Ella and Audrey laugh.

"On a completely different note, but still speaking of men, Julie tells me you ran into Carter several nights ago at dinner."

"Yeah."

"And—"

Ella chuckles. "He was very nice. He bought dinner for Julie, Sophia, and me."

"Is that all?"

"He sent me a text saying it was nice to see me and he'd like to get together in a week or so when he returns from an out-of-town recording session."

"What do you think you'll do?"

"I'll meet with him. See what he wants."

"Do you think he's changed?"

Ella shrugs.

"I think it's wonderful for you to be out and about. That's also important for healing. However, be careful, dear. Remember, Carter hurt you and acted like a bit of a jerk."

"I know. I'll be careful. I have a better perspective about him now. Besides, I really am getting out and about."

"Oh?"

"I have a date on Monday."

"Really? With whom?" Audrey, excited, is all ears.

"Harrison Grant. Julie and I stopped for gas, and we ran into him."

"Didn't you and Sophia double date with Harrison and his brother, Luke, a while back?"

"It wasn't actually a double date . . . just a spur-of-the-moment thing after Harrison put up the pergola on my back patio. We went to dinner and a concert in the park."

"He didn't ask you for a date right after?"

"You know how life is, Mom. You say, 'Let's get together,' and then work, life, and everything gets in the way."

"So, tell me more about Harrison."

Ella chuckles. "He's tall with beautiful, friendly blue eyes, and very manly. He used to work on Wall Street but traded it in for another life. He's in business with his father and brother—Grant and Sons Construction."

"Oh, I know that company. I've seen their trucks around town and ads in the newspaper. Has he ever been married?"

"Engaged, but it didn't work out."

Audrey gazes at Ella, who chuckles, aware of her mother's insatiable curiosity for more details.

"I don't know much else, Mom, but I'll give you a full report after Monday."

"You better." Audrey stirs the sauce, simmering on the stove. "Sweetie, I think the sauce is ready; you can assemble the chicken parmesan while I set the dining room table."

Ella preheats the oven to 350 degrees F. She removes the plate of breaded chicken breasts from the fridge, along with a package of individually sliced Provolone cheese, and places them on the kitchen counter. Next, she removes a large glass tray from a side cabinet next to the stove.

At the counter, she spoons out a generous portion of fragrant tomato sauce, covering the bottom of the dish, and places the breaded chicken breasts on top. After she adds another layer of sauce over the chicken, she covers the top of the dish with cheese and pops it in the oven to bake.

"Let's see," begins Audrey, looking at the wall clock. "The table is set—"

"I just put the chicken parm in the oven," says Ella. "The salad is in the fridge, minus the dressing, until we serve it."

"Okay, then." Audrey heads toward the breadbasket on the counter. "I'll slice the baguette to make the garlic bread. Would you be a dear and place the Brie and crackers on a plate? I also cut up some veggies for the crudité, and we have hummus."

"Sure, Mom. I'll get that ready and place the platters in the great room."

Some twenty minutes later, the doorbell rings, and in the next instant, Ella's thirty-four-year-old brother, Justin, can be heard at the front door. He enters with his pretty girlfriend, Heather. Justin, a tall, GQ-looking ER doc with a head of neatly cropped dark hair, met Heather, a nurse and caregiver, when one of Heather's patients had a medical emergency. The two hit it off almost immediately and have been dating for over a year. Ella would not be surprised if, one day soon, they make an engagement announcement.

Julie, holding a bottle of cabernet, and Tom, a bag of garden vegetables, enter moments later. A round of hellos and kisses and hugs ensues.

"Oh, my, these veggies are gorgeous!" gushes Audrey, captivated by the vibrant colors and fresh aroma of the garden vegetables and herbs.

"We have more produce in our greenhouse than we can use, so feel free to call for deliveries."

"I made the tomato sauce we're having today with the Roma tomatoes, garlic, and basil you brought last week," Audrey tells them.

"I sampled the sauce," says Ella, who then touches her hand to her lips, kisses it, and flips her fingers with flair in the classic Italian gesture. "*Perfecto!*"

"I hope you like my German chocolate brownies," says Heather, holding a large tin.

Audrey laughs. "My dear, we are all confessed chocoholics in this family." She takes the brownies from Heather and places them on the dining room credenza next to the lemon-ricotta pie.

"Guilty," claims Ella.

"Ditto." Julie raises her hand.

"Me three." Michael laughs.

"Me four," says Justin. "I made Heather give me one to sample on the way over. Don't worry, Mom, I'll eat all my dinner and dessert, too." He rubs his stomach playfully.

"Please," says Audrey, motioning for everyone to sit down. "Help yourself to some appetizers. But not too many—we'll be eating dinner shortly."

After Michael takes drink orders ranging from soft drinks to wine, the family converses until dinner is served. The conversation ranges from the new waiting-area garden installed at the hospital where Justin works, to Michael's hole-in-one win on the golf course, extended family news, and Ella's upcoming party plans with Sophia at their Firefly Lane Farm Catering and Events facility.

"Say, Julie, did they ever find those kids destroying all the Main Street holiday lights?" Michael asks.

"We have some clues, thanks to social media catching footage of some of the acts. No faces were visible, however. The culprits carefully protected their identity, but we're still investigating."

Audrey sighs. "What a shame that kids would be so cruel."

"It is," Ella replies. "Young kids, however, sometimes get pressured to follow the pack. I'm wondering if they realize the impact of their actions."

"Well, I know they don't comprehend the consequences," says

Tom.

"Christmas means so much more than the lights, presents, and festivities. At mass today, the priest talked about how we shouldn't lose sight of the deeper meaning—the blessing of our Lord coming to Earth to save humanity from sin and to take away the penalty of eternal punishment, showing us by example how we should live—*doing unto others.*"

"I wonder if the kids destroying these properties and causing grief to so many realize the magnitude of their actions," Heather adds.

"Probably not. The kids probably haven't a clue as to the real meaning of Christmas or how we're meant to treat one another. Instead, they get some cruel pleasure out of destruction or causing havoc, and that's why they continue," answers Julie.

"I wonder what in their lives makes them lack empathy." Ella sighs.

"I don't know," Julie shakes her head. I'll tell you what I do know, though—we'll find out."

Later that evening, Ella sits in the great room by the twinkling lights on her Christmas tree as she ponders her lunch date with Harrison the next day. What to wear?

Harrison usually wears jeans. I could wear jeans, but for a first date, maybe black slacks, my black boots with the nice heel and, considering the upcoming holiday, a red turtleneck with my gold hoop earrings and my creamy black leather jacket. Casual but classy and feminine. Okay, that's settled.

Next, Ella's mind turns to Carter—how good he makes her feel and how he knows just the right words to say. But can she trust him this time around? Has he had a change of heart? Does he want something more—like a real, lasting relationship? With the uncertainty about Carter's intentions and the fear of being hurt again, her mind swirls with thoughts.

Truth be told, she is deeply attracted to both men. Each possesses a unique charm that captivates her, their presence a constant in her thoughts.

"Stop," she tells herself. "Take it one day at a time. Don't let your thoughts run wild." It's a mantra she repeats, a steady rhythm to guide her through the uncertainty.

Ella gazes at the beautiful, vintage Holy Family tree topper and marvels at its beauty. She is grateful for her blessings. When she thinks of all the local vandalism and unhappy souls, she prays for peace and an end to crime and disharmony in town. Silently, she asks the Lord for what she feels would be a miracle—to change the hearts of the teens causing so much damage and anxiety.

And Lord, I humbly ask for your guidance in my romantic life to lead me to my perfect mate. Your will be done.

As she prays, a surge of warm sensations permeates her body, and she feels that the Lord has answered her prayer.

Thank you, Father.

A New Day

"Every moment is a fresh beginning."

~~T.S. Eliot

Chapter Six

_____

"Hey, good morning, girlfriend." With a coffee mug in hand, Sophia steps into Ella's office. "What time did you get in?"

"Eight or so."

"Why so early?"

Ella smiles broadly like a Cheshire cat, prompting Sophia to take on the role of investigative reporter.

"So? Tell me. You heard from Carter, right?"

"Yes, but that's not it."

"What? What do you mean?" Sophia sits in a chair facing Ella's large wood desk.

"Carter said he enjoyed seeing me this weekend but that he's going out of town to finish recording his new album. He says he'd like to together again when he returns."

"Really? I don't know about him. He didn't treat you so well—"

"I've got Carter's number now. I don't know what he'll say or what to expect, but I'm willing to listen. I don't hold any hard feelings. I probably understand his fears and where he's coming from more than he does."

"I've got to hand it to you. You act with such grace."

Ella chuckles, her Cheshire cat smile is back.

"So then, why else are you smiling?"

"Ha!" yells Ella. "What makes you think I've got anything else to share?"

"How many years have I known you?"

Ella giggles. "Too many."

"Look at you turning red. So, who is _he?_"

Ella bursts out laughing at Sophia's inquiry. "I have a noon lunch date with *Harrison Grant.*"

Sophia whistles. "Okay then, busted. Details, please."

"Julie and I ran into him by chance over the weekend. He took my number and texted me later asking for a lunch date. He's picking me up at the office and taking me to that new place, The Cottage Dining and Reading Room."

"And I'm just learning about this *now*?"

Ella chuckles again. "I heard from him late Saturday and was busy at my folks yesterday. I figured I'd tell you this morning."

"Hmmm. Well, next time anything juicy happens, I want to hear about it pronto."

"Yes, ma'am." Ella salutes Sophia, and the two friends break out in laughter.

The hours fly by as Ella meets with prospective clients who want to tour Firefly Lane Farm's on-site event space for future wedding and party bookings. She is thankful the morning is sunny and warmer than usual. With the snow from the recent flurries melting, guests can imagine the views during spring, summer, and fall.

Firefly Lane Farm is a unique property and venue on ten stunning acres with expertly tended fruit, flower, and vegetable gardens. The farm is also home to Sophia, who lives in a charming, single-story Cape Cod-style home with a gabled roof. The newly renovated barn houses Ella and Sophia's catering and event business headquarters, which boasts a phenomenal event hall and kitchen. Other spectacular property features include a winery, vineyard, outdoor event space, and gathering area with an overhead roof and wood-and-stone kitchen overlooking panoramic views of the Peconic Bay's impressive acreage and still waters.

At noon on the dot, Ella hears Harrison's "Hello" and turns from her computer screen, which faces the vineyard and Bay.

"Hi!" Ella smiles warmly, matching Harrison's greeting.

Harrison, who typically dons casual denim jeans and a T-shirt or velour zip-up, has made a striking change for his lunch date with Ella. He now sports an elegant navy blue and white roll-neck sweater adorned with a handsome geometric design at the collar. His beautiful head of thick, silky, dark, wavy hair and sparkling eyes catch Ella's attention.

Ella, filled with anticipation, rises from her desk and gracefully moves towards her coat and bag, resting on a nearby chair.

"You look great," acknowledges Harrison. "Red becomes you."

"Thank you. I like your sweater. It accents the color of your eyes," replies Ella coyly.

A bit more animated than usual, Sophia suddenly appears at Ella's office door. At the same time, Harrison turns to greet her. Ella mouths "behave" to Sophia.

"So, where are you two having lunch?" asks Sophia, already knowing the answer.

"The Cottage Dining and Reading Room," answers Harrison.

"Oh, the new place in town. It looks adorable from the outside. Let me know how you both like it."

"We will," Harrison promises.

"Well, enjoy. I'm off to meet with our sommelier to go over wine ideas for our next farm-to-table dinner," says Sophia, taking her leave.

"I'm parked right out front," Harrison tells Ella as they walk toward the barn's entrance. Outside, he opens the passenger door of his Range Rover to allow Ella to take her seat, immediately putting her at ease. Ella likes it when a man opens her door. "The Cottage has quite a menu, everything from breakfast fare to three-course meals," Harrison says as he pulls away from the curb.

"I looked online. It looks charming and has received rave reviews."

"It was a residential property also zoned for commercial uses. Our company renovated the home and brought it up to code for a restaurant venue."

"Really? I love the look—modern farmhouse."

"It is all the rage."

Getting caught up on their work lives and town happenings, by the time Harrison and Ella arrive at their destination, the flow of conversation is light and natural, each putting the other at ease.

ONCE UPON A COVE CHRISTMAS

"Ooh, I like it," gushes Ella, entering from the cottage landing with its wrap-around porch. Inside, a welcoming reception area adorned with white shiplap on the walls and accent colors in various shades of sand and blue, make a serene statement. From the entrance, a wall of French doors overlooks the grounds out to the bay. Modern wood pendant lights hang inside the dining room from a high-pitched, natural wood-beam ceiling. Tables and comfortable booths are constructed with reclaimed wood and cream-colored upholstered benches and chairs. Hanging greenery provides more organic, natural elements.

"Right this way." The young hostess shows Ella and Harrison to their comfortable booth.

"The ambiance is so cozy and elegant."

"Thank you." Harrison smiles.

His gorgeous blue eyes drink in Ella, and as they do, she feels a surge of electricity course through her body. Her intuition tells her that Harrison is a special man.

In the next instant, a waiter visits their table, offers them both menus, and takes their beverage orders. Ella orders a sugar-free iced tea and Harrison, an Arnold Palmer.

"Everything looks so delicious." Ella peruses the menu and debates over selecting the salad of farmhouse greens with heirloom tomatoes paired with a choice of grilled fish or chicken or the day's special—striped bass with a lemon crème sauce, julienne vegetables, and sweet basil rice, which comes with a choice of soup or a mixed green salad.

"It's going to be the special for me." Harrison grins as he places his menu on the side of the table. "I'll have the striped bass too. It sounds delicious and different from the fish I usually cook."

The waiter places a breadbasket on Ella and Harrison's table and takes their lunch order—two striped bass specials served with farmhouse salads.

"So, you enjoy cooking?" Harrison lifts the napkin on the breadbasket and surveys the warm rolls and seasoned focaccia bread selection.

"Love it." Ella examines the freshly baked breads and selects a rosemary-lavender roll. Harrison chooses a slice of roasted focaccia. He drizzles his bread plate with the Cottage's signature Myer lemon-infused olive oil.

"What's your specialty?"

Ella tears off a piece of her roll, swirls it around in a small sea of oil, and pops it into her mouth before she answers. "I'd have to say Italian, Indian, vegetarian, and vegan. I love to come up with healthy fare—lots of fresh, organic veggies and produce mixed with tasty herbs and spices.

Harrison chuckles. "Well, I'll offer my services as a taste tester if you ever need one."

Ella loves how Harrison's entire face lights up when he smiles. He has a good vibe. For the next twenty minutes, the banter between the two of them is light and carefree.

"You're probably wondering why, after we went to that concert in the park with Sophia and my brother, Luke, I didn't call," Harrison comments, taking a more serious tone.

Ella looks up from her plate, smiles, and waits for Harrison to continue.

"I, we . . . well, things got a bit crazy with work, and truth be told, I was a little nervous about asking you out."

"You were?" Ella is amazed.

Harrison nods. "I wasn't sure if I was ready to open up to someone I was attracted to and was beginning to have feelings for."

Ella is astonished at Harrison's reveal and doesn't quite know how to respond. She takes a forkful of vegetables and rice, her mind racing with a mix of surprise and curiosity. "I see."

"Then, when we saw each other that day at the gas station. I knew I wanted to get to know you better and see if we had potential. To share a secret, I haven't dated much since my engagement ended. So, I'm a little rusty."

"You were engaged?" Ella asks the question even though she's heard the answer through the town grapevine.

"Yes. We broke up a few months before I met you."

"Please, let me know if I'm getting too personal, but what happened?"

"Lisa, that was her name. I found her cheating on me with my best buddy, Jim."

"Oh, no. I'm so sorry."

Harrison shakes his head. "So was I. It was a hard pill to swallow. I lost two people I cared about in one fell swoop."

"How did you find out?"

"Instinct. Without going into the gory details, I found some telltale signs and put two and two together. Worse than that, I learned that Jim wasn't the first."

"Are they still together?"

"They dated for a while. I was told Lisa moved back to her hometown in Texas. I haven't spoken to her or seen Jim since." Harrison takes a sip of his Arnold Palmer. "What about you? You had mentioned that your husband passed away."

Ella nods. "In a plane crash. He was coming to Lavender Hill Cove to repair our marriage."

"Oh?"

"I haven't shared this with many people, so, between you and me, here's my secret—my husband wanted a divorce—mid-life crisis perhaps? Anyway, he had a change of heart, and I was willing to work on things, but . . . then there was the crash."

Harrison reaches for Ella's hand. She takes it in hers, and they share a heartfelt smile.

"I guess we all have our crosses." Harrison squeezes her hand before they both let go and resume eating.

Turning to a lighter conversation topic, Ella tells Harrison about the latest in the upcoming Once Upon a Cove Christmas Gala, detailing the theme and some activities planned.

"I know the librarian, Doris Banks," Harrison says as he sips on his drink.

"You do?"

Harrison nods. "Our paths cross again, Ella. Doris had Grant and Sons draw up the architectural plans for the library's new wing."

"Seriously?"

Harrison nods.

"What a small world!"

"Indeed."

Ella takes another forkful of her salad, amused at life's synchronicities.

"What do you want for your life, moving forward?" Harrison asks to move the conversation along.

"Continue with my business, settle down with my special someone who shares the same family values, have some kids, and a good life minus the drama. You?"

"Ditto."

"Here's to living the good life with love, laughter, and minus the drama," Harrison says, and he and Ella clink their glasses.

After discussing their hobbies—Ella's antiquing, decorating, crafting, working out, cooking, and entertaining; Harrison's woodworking, gardening, boating, water sports, skiing, and watching selected sports on television with his brother, Luke, to name a few—Harrison pays the lunch bill.

"I really enjoyed lunch," says Harrison as he walks with Ella back to his SUV.

"Me too."

"Want to do this again?"

Ella nods with a smile.

"Saturday, if you're free? The Water's Edge in Jamesport has great food and live music. I could make a reservation for dinner."

"I'd love that." When Harrison accidentally brushes against Ella, an electric surge goes through her body. The moment quickly dissipates when a cacophony of foreboding sounds rises in the distance just as Harrison opens the passenger door of his SUV for Ella.

"Help! Catch those kids!" they hear a man scream.

Ella and Harrison quickly rush around to the back of the SUV to see what the commotion is about.

"They stole a case of my best whiskey!" The man, who looks to be in his sixties, is standing beside a large delivery truck.

Harrison scans the parking lot. In the distance, running frantically, a group of what looks to be teenage boys wearing jeans and dark hoodies head toward a black sedan. Harrison takes off in hot pursuit. However, with their head start, the boys pile into the car, which screeches away down the deserted country road.

Harrison motions "just a minute" to Ella and quickly opens the door to his SUV. He removes a pen and pad from the center console and writes down a license plate number.

"You got their plate?" Ella is astonished.

"Yup," says Harrison proudly. "I think we should call the police."

"I'll call Julie!" Ella immediately pulls her cell phone from her bag and hits the speed dial for her sister. Harrison hands her the pad with the license plate.

Once Ella gives Julie the details, Ella looks at Harrison. "Julie's asking us to come to the station to fill out a report."

Moments later, the truck driver approaches Harrison and Ella.

"Just a moment, Julie. Hang on," Ella says into the phone. "Hi, sir, my name is Ella Martin."

"And I'm Harrison Grant."

"My name's Ben Long. Did you happen to get their plate number?"

"I did," says Grant as Ella listens to her sister on the line.

"I'm on the phone with my sister," Ella tells him. "She works for the Lavender Hill Cove Police and would like us all to come in to give our statements. Can you do that?"

"Sure," says Ben.

When Harrison nods, Ella says, "Okay, then. Sis, we're on our way to you now."

"Follow us, Ben," Harrison instructs. Ben gives a thumbs up.

Angels Among Us

"Every good and perfect gift is from above."

(James 1:17)

Chapter Seven

"The boys were all wearing masks and hoodies; I honestly can't tell you much more." Ben sighs and runs his hands through his gray hair. He sits on the sofa in Julie's office at the Lavender Hill Cove Police Department headquarters next to Harrison. Ella and Julie sit on chairs directly facing the men.

"Are you sure?" asks Julie, scribbling on a notepad. "Let's go through the details once more. Visualize them in your mind's eye."

"Okay. I was unloading crates of wine and other liquors onto my dolly. I make my delivery to the Cottage every other Monday. I was inside my truck, and I saw these kids, three boys—I would say they were in their mid-teens—in varying heights, all wearing jeans, dark hoodies, and ski masks. They were helping themselves to my crates. I started yelling, and just as I was getting off the back of my truck onto the pavement, the last kid picked up a crate. Wait—he a had a *tattoo*—a skull and cross bones—on the back of his right hand." Ben points to the dorsal side of his hand.

"Wow. Julie, just like the boy who stole Doris's and Louise's handbags that day."

"Hmm." Julie ponders this new development. "Well, thank you all for your statements. I'll be in touch if I have any other questions."

"Anything more I can do, let me know." Ben stands and shakes Julie's hand, followed by Harrison's and Ella's, before exiting Julie's office.

"What next?" asks Ella.

"I'm going to head over to Lavender Hill Cove High School and do some snooping. What about you two?"

"I've got appointments starting at three," states Harrison.

"I need to get back to work too," Ella adds.

"Ella, I'll give you a ring later." Julie gives her sister a peck on the cheek. "Harrison, always a pleasure." She shakes Harrison's hand.

"I know at lunch we talked about no drama, but—" Harrison chuckles as he and Ella sit in his SUV parked in from of the Firefly Lane Farm offices. "However, despite all the excitement, I enjoyed being with you."

"I liked being with you too." Ella smiles warmly.

Harrison reaches for her hand, which is resting on the center console, brings it to his lips, and kisses it. His lips, tender and soft, make Ella's temperature rise a few degrees. She naturally leans into him, and the two share a quick kiss.

"See you Saturday at six p.m.," says Ella as she opens the car door.

"I'll call you before then though. Enjoy the rest of your afternoon." Harrison pulls his SUV away from the curb as Ella waves.

"Sounds like you and Harrison got more than you bargained for at lunch today. I'm sure all this vandalism, etcetera, is a group of out-of-control teens, and Julie and her department will have answers soon. But enough about that, let's get to the good stuff. How was lunch?" asks Sophia with a playful lilt. She stands against the doorframe of Ella's office.

"I don't kiss and tell." Ella, sitting at her desk, bats her eyelashes playfully.

"Oh? Can I bribe you with some pumpkin-chocolate chip muffins?" Sophia holds up a bag from the Love Street Bakery.

"You didn't?"

"I did." Sophia waves the bag of pastries before Ella.

"I told you I can't resist them," whines Ella. "I'm trying to pace myself for the holidays."

In defiance, Sophia removes a spectacularly large muffin from the bag and takes a bite. She moans with delight as she chews.

Ella starts to laugh. "Okay, okay. Let's make some tea and split one of those mammoth muffins, and I'll fill you in.

Sophia gives Ella a thumbs up.

"Harrison's a true gentleman," reveals Ella as she and Sophia make teas in the office kitchen. He opened my car door, pulled out my chair, and ensured I was happy with my meal. He also asked me for a date on Saturday."

"Wow, so it did go well."

With tea mugs in hand, the two sit at a small, round, wood kitchen table where the sliced muffin halves sit on a pretty china plate.

"Where's he taking you?"

"To The Water's Edge for dinner and live music."

"Nice. *And?*"

"And . . . *I like him.* I want to know more, but it feels good."

"You deserve it. Enjoy."

Later that afternoon, as Ella pulls into her driveway, she notices that the Robinsons' "For Sale" sign is down. An elegant gray-haired woman, wearing jeans and a parka, her hair in a long braid down her back, is filling a bird feeder hanging from the porch ceiling.

Curious, Ella parks her car in her garage and makes her way over to the woman next door. "Hello," she calls and waves.

"Hello," replies the woman cheerily.

"My name's Ella Martin. I live next door," Ella adds as she approaches the porch landing.

"Mine's Rosemary Engel. It's a pleasure to meet you." Rosemary's face lights up with a warmth that makes Ella feel instantly at ease. Ella tries to guess her age but can't pinpoint it. Although the woman appears older, she has gorgeous, smooth, luminescent skin and blue eyes that radiate warmth. Rosemary has a genuine and peaceful demeanor.

"Did you buy the Robinsons' house?"

"Oh, no, dear, I'm just here temporarily."

"I see." Rosemary's answer catches Ella off guard. She thought the Robinsons were selling. It's probably difficult for them to sell their home during the holidays, she decides. Ella doesn't want to pry. "You must have moved in when I was at work. I didn't see any moving vans."

Rosemary doesn't answer, only smiles.

"Do you think you'll get many birds coming your way?" Ella points to the bird feeder. "I love watching the winter birds."

"I've seen several red cardinals."

"How lovely. They're my favorite."

"Mine, too."

"I'm happy to meet you. Please feel free to knock on my door or call me if you need anything or have any questions about the neighborhood." Ella hands Rosemary her card.

"I appreciate that."

Ella waves goodbye and heads back to her house. For the next two hours, she returns client texts and vendor emails, folds two loads of laundry, and tends to several other household tasks. Only when her stomach grumbles does she think about dinner, and then her cell phone rings.

"Hello, dear. It's Rosemary. Have you eaten dinner yet? I made some New England clam chowder and cornbread. Would you like to join me?"

"That sounds perfect. I was contemplating what to make. Thank you. Can I bring anything?"

"Just yourself. Come now if you'd like."

Once the call ends, Ella, never wanting to accept a dinner invitation and arrive empty-handed, heads to her kitchen pantry and grabs a bottle of Firefly Lane Farm's best chardonnay.

"Rosemary, it looks like you've lived here for years," marvels Ella as she scans the expertly decorated L-shaped living/dining/kitchen area. The space is comfortable, beachy, and elegant in white, blue, and sandy tones. "You even decorated for Christmas."

"Of course, it's the most wonderful time of year," gushes Rosemary. Ella notes a beautifully decorated tree in one corner and a painted porcelain figurine of the Holy Family on the mantle above the stone fireplace.

Rosemary sets out a cheese-and-fruit platter on the great room's coffee table. "Thank you for the wine." She admires the label's pretty country scene. "Firefly Lane Farm Chardonnay. Lovely artwork."

"Thank you. My friend, Sophia Abrams, owns Firefly Lane Farm, and we're partners in Firefly Lane Farm Catering and Events."

"I'd like to hear all about it. Please, make yourself at home. Would you like a glass of wine? I also have iced tea, or I could warm up some homemade apple cider."

"Oh, hot apple cider would be wonderful. I haven't had that since I was a kid," Ella replies as she checks out the impressive art collection on Rosemary's walls. "Speaking of artwork just now, these paintings are gorgeous." Ella admires a mix of oils on canvas and beautifully framed photos depicting a variety of country settings and beach scenes.

"Here you go." Rosemary sets two mugs of steaming cider on coasters on the great room's attractive wood coffee table and sits on the adjacent loveseat. "I like to paint and do photography."

"These are your works?" asks Ella. She sits on the sofa opposite Rosemary and blows on her cider before sipping.

Rosemary nods. "Painting and photography are two of my great joys. I love capturing God's beauty in nature."

"Well, you certainly have quite a talent."

"Thank you, my dear. Tell me about yourself and more about what you do."

"Ever since I can remember, I've loved cooking and entertaining. My family is big on inviting friends and family over for get-togethers. That's probably why I chose a career as an event planner. I organize all types of gatherings—weddings, anniversaries, retirement parties, and other celebrations. I had been living in Los Angeles, but after my husband passed in a plane crash—"

"I'm sorry, dear."

"Thank you. After Jack passed, I decided to stay in Lavender Hill Cove. I grew up here, and Sophia—well, her husband died several years ago. She needed help with the farm, and I needed a job, so one thing led to another, and we formed our catering and events company. It's been very cathartic and profitable, and we enjoy working together." Ella pauses to take a sip of cider. "Where are you from?"

"Oh, here and there. I've held various jobs assisting people with this and that," answers Rosemary with a twinkle in her eye.

"What brought you to Lavender Hill Cove?"

"I'd have to say destiny—God's will." Rosemary chuckles. "I've always loved living by the water in the country near lots of trees and flowers and open spaces."

"Ditto on that." Ella holds up her mug, and she and Rosemary toast.

"Hungry?"

"Yes."

"Me too. Come, let's eat."

Ella follows Rosemary into the dining room, and they continue to become acquainted over the next few hours. Rosemary is exceptional, possessing a unique mystique and Ella can't help but enjoy the woman's motherly way and the feeling that she has known Rosemary all her life.

"How did your visit to Lavender Hill Cove High School go today, Sis?" asks Ella later that evening. In her PJs, Ella holds her cell phone to her ear as she lies stretched out on her bed in the dark.

"Nothing concrete yet, but I'll keep you posted."

For the next twenty minutes, Ella fills Julie in on her lunch date with Harrison, followed by another dinner with her new neighbor, Rosemary. "Sis," Ella says with a yawn. "I can barely keep my eyes open. Talk to you tomorrow?"

"Sleep tight," Julie replies before hanging up.

Within five minutes, Ella is sound asleep.

In her dream, Ella sees male figures in dark clothing. They laugh and holler as they break store windows and destroy holiday decorations.

"Hey! Stop it!" screams Ella at the top of her lungs. When the boys see her, they run, and Ella runs after them. However, the boys separate and run in different directions. She follows one of the boys but loses him.

Next, in the snow ahead of where she stands, Ella sees a dark object. She realizes it's a wallet, picks it up, and opens the leather cover.

Ella wakes with a start, disturbed that she didn't see the wallet's contents.

What a strange dream. What does it mean?

However, when her morning alarm chimes seconds later, indicating it's time to get ready for work, all thoughts of the dream fall by the wayside as Ella prepares for her day.

"You're up bright and early, Rosemary!" Ella yells out her car window as she backs down the driveway headed to work.

"Every morning."

"Thank you again for dinner last night. Next time, you'll have to come over to my place."

"I'd love that. Headed to the office?"

Ella nods and waves goodbye.

It's a gorgeous day. Although the temperature on the car's

dashboard says it's 45 degrees, the snow on the ground from the recent flurries has melted, leaving only mounds of frozen snow in clumps along the sides of the road. The sun's rays are warm and bright.

"Thank you, Lord, for this beautiful day." Ella breathes deeply, soaking up all the beautiful country visuals as she travels down the two-lane road—the still blue waters of the Peconic on one side, stately Victorian and Colonial homes, picturesque barns, and miles and miles of farmland on the other side.

Ella's cell phone rings and Carter's name pops up on the car's console. Her heart skips a beat as she presses the green button to answer the phone. "This is Ella."

Since transitioning into her own business, Ella has developed the habit of answering her phone as if she's always at her office desk. With no landline, except for one designated phone at the Firefly Lane Farm office, her cell phone is now used for both personal and professional purposes. Although she knows it's Carter on the other end of the line, she doesn't want to appear too eager.

"Hi, Ella, Carter here. How are you?"

"Doing well," answers Ella casually.

"I'm almost finished recording the album, and I'll definitely be back in town next week. If you're free, I'd love to take you to dinner. Maybe Friday night?"

Ella and Carter converse until Ella arrives at her office. Again, she wonders what Carter wants from her and if he's had second thoughts about becoming involved. Her thoughts start to swirl.

Is that what I want now? What about Harrison?

"Can I get back to you, Carter? I'm in the car now, and I'd like to check my calendar."

After a busy morning meeting with pre-scheduled vendors—two florists and a printer—and giving tours to two prospective clients, one interested in a wedding venue, another for a fiftieth anniversary celebration, Ella grabs lunch with Sophia in the barn's kitchen.

"So, will you go out with him?" asks Sophia, as she and Ella share a salad and leftover spinach-and-mushroom quiche.

"What do you think?"

"He's not my favorite person after leaving you in the dust."

"I know, but I'd like to hear him out—and then there's Harrison."

"My motto is until both parties agree to date exclusively, all is fair in love and war. Besides, you're finding things out and what works best for you. I'll support you in whatever you decide. But if either Harrison or Carter hurt you, I can't say I won't seek revenge. It will be me that your detective sister will be investigating." Sophia laughs. "Say, did Julie ever find any information about the kid with the tattoo that stole the liquor?"

"As of last night, no, but she's working on it." Ella sighs as she ponders ideas. "I wish we could do more to build positive community spirit and goodwill."

"Let's think about it, but only for a bit."

"With only four weeks until our fundraiser gala, besides selling tickets to the gathering and wrangling up silent auction items benefiting the library and the local retailers—" Ella continues to think and then a lightbulb moment—"Maybe we could contact more sponsors and donors—ones that will write checks to support the cause. A selling point can be that we'll incorporate them into the press releases and media we generate before, during, and post-event."

"Great idea! The Old Town Bank has been a big supporter of Firefly Lane Farm through the years. I've got a good contact that I can phone," adds Sophia. "I've been adding to the Excel list of high-profile donors in our shared drive. I'll also write a letter to send out as soon as possible."

"Maybe we can also network with the local country clubs," suggests Ella. "Oh, I heard back from the Knights of Columbus. I meant to tell you earlier, but you were on the phone. They're on board with providing several auction items. I'll call them back. Maybe they might want to make a cash donation, too."

"Woo-hoo!" yells Sophia, clapping. "This event keeps on growing with more definition."

"By next year, we'll have it down to a science."

"What's our guest list at now?"

"Two forty-four, but the RSVPs keep rolling in, and we still have four more weeks until the gala."

"The fire marshal approved the event space to hold four hundred, so we're getting there."

"Hey, maybe I can ask Carter to play?" asks Ella off the cuff.

"Oh, that is *genius*! That would boost ticket sales one hundred percent! I knew he was good for something!"

"Now, *be nice*."

"Sorry. *Not*!" Sophia laughs.

"You're incorrigible."

"True. But you love me anyway. Chocolate?" Sophia rips into a giant chocolate bar laden with salted almonds and coconut.

"Oh, yeah." Ella holds out her hand for a piece of the candy bar and promptly bites off a chunk. "Yum."

"From Lavender Hill Cove Gourmet Treats."

"Make sure they put this bar in the gift baskets they donate for the silent auction. This chocolate is killer."

"Already on it," says Sophia, munching on a candy wedge.

Sophia and Ella continue to tend to the details for the Once Upon a Cove Christmas Gala, for the next few hours.

"The decor will be reminiscent of Victorian England, in line with Charles Dicken's 'A Christmas Carol.' And carolers will greet guests over here as they arrive." Ella points to where the carolers will be stationed as she and Sophia peruse the barn's foyer and hall. "Inside the hall, there'll be round tables for ten set white cloths, red napkins, glistening white china, and silverware. The centerpieces will be winter greenery, white candles, and red poinsettias. On either side of the stage, there'll be beautifully decorated trees with sparkling white lights and silver, gold, and glass ornaments, and the stage backdrop will depict a Victorian city street at Christmas."

"Absolutely divine!" Sophia exclaims with enthusiasm. "I've arranged for a dance floor to be placed in front of the stage so people can dance."

"The Seagull's manager left word earlier that they're available for the event," adds Sophia regarding the popular local band they've invited to play at the gala. "I'll call back to discuss the band's fee."

"Works for me."

"Oh, and I've also left word with DJ Cory Michaels to see if he'll act as MC. His involvement could really elevate the event," Sophia says.

"I'm confident the gala will be a resounding success. I can feel it in my bones." Ella smiles, her excitement palpable.

Boys will be Boys

"Walk with the wise and you become wise,

but the companion of fools fares badly."

(Proverbs 13:20)

Chapter Eight

After a quick stop at the local grocery store to purchase a few items—mixed lettuce, a cucumber, and Roma tomatoes, as well as a few extra food staples to get her through the week before the usual weekend grocery spree—Ella heads home with dinner on her mind. At least once a month, she makes a hearty and delicious pasta sauce from canned crushed tomatoes, tomato paste, sautéed onions, garlic, and a host of fresh seasonings, to which she adds sweet Italian sausage and meatballs from her family's recipe. Adding the meatballs and sausage into the sauce to simmer and marinate for a time creates a blend of ingredients so delectable that it has become one of her favorite comfort meals. The sauce and meat get portioned out for small meals—one a week throughout the month—and frozen until intended use. For tonight's dinner, the last installment of her sauce-making session sits thawing in the refrigerator.

Knowing tonight's portion is enough for two people, Ella, spur of the moment, decides she will phone Rosemary shortly to see if she might want to join her for dinner.

At the entrance to her driveway, Ella leans out of the car window and open's the mailbox to retrieve the day's delivery: a utility bill, an early Christmas card from cousins living on the Cape, and many junk advertisements. Suddenly, she hears a loud male voice issuing an order, "Let's get out of here. The lights just went on!"

Ella quickly surveys her home—the bushes near the porch entry, strung with white lights, sparkle. No one is in the vicinity. However, hearing more distant yells to vacate the premises, seemingly coming from a distance, Ella turns her head toward Rosemary's property and sees Rosemary on her porch landing yelling at several hooded figures making their getaway.

"Rosemary!" Ella screams as she exits her car and runs toward her friend. Once Ella approaches Rosemary's front lawn, she notices that the poor baby Jesus, taken out of the manger, lies face down on the ground, as do the Blessed Mother, St. Joseph, and the three Magi. The hay from the manger is strewn about the snow, and the string of white lights decorating the manger is rolled up in a ball on the ground.

"Who would want to do such a thing?" Rosemary asks incredulously, meeting Ella at the manger. For a few moments, the women assess the carnage.

"What's this?" Ella bends down to pick up what appears to be a black leather wallet half buried in the snow.

"Adam Black is the name on the library card," says Ella, scouring the wallet for other identification. "And on his ID. There's also an address, Five Meadow Lane."

"That's not too far from here," Rosemary points out.

"There's a twenty-five-dollar gift card to Joe's Sporting Goods, some baseball cards, and ten dollars and change. No driver's license, so probably a young teen."

Rosemary sighs, inspecting the manger. "Well, thank goodness, it doesn't look like they did any real damage. Just overturned statues, strewn hay, and lights that need to be put back in place."

"I wonder if Adam here and his buddies are the kids terrorizing the town."

"What could they possibly have against Christmas?"

"Beats me. Maybe all they've gotten from Santa is coal in their stockings. If it's okay with you, I'll call my sister, Julie. She's been investigating all the vandalism cases."

"Please. Let's get to the bottom of this."

"How many boys did you notice?" Julie asks Rosemary. She sits taking notes on an oversized chair opposite the sofa where Rosemary and Ella are seated.

"There were three figures, dressed in black and they wore ski masks so I couldn't see their faces. But I heard them yelling and scrambling after I turned the porch light on. They all sounded like young boys."

"I also saw what appeared to be three boys, and I heard one of them yell, 'Let's get out of here!'" adds Ella.

After Julie finishes taking their statements, Ella asks, "What's next?"

"My associate and I are going to visit Adam Black's home," Julie states.

"These boys definitely need a talking to, but no real damage has been done. I'd like to speak with them," says Rosemary.

"We'll have to take that one step at a time. If these are the same boys involved in the town's recent crimes, vandalism falls under the category of a misdemeanor offense, and depending upon the circumstances and damages, as well as prior convictions, these actions would fall under the criminal mischief category and may be punishable by prison time."

"Oh, dear." Rosemary shakes her head sorrowfully, thinking more about the boys' futures than her property.

"I'll keep you both posted," Julie says, closing her notepad.

The following day at work, Ella gets a notification that twenty-eight more couples have registered for the gala, bringing the total number of attendees to 300. Ella remains confident that they'll reach a total capacity of 400.

"Hi." Harrison's friendly voice on her cell phone gives Ella the afternoon pick-me-up she needs. "How's your day going?"

After sharing their day's news, Harrison lets Ella know that he and his brother, Luke, would like to purchase a table of ten for the holiday gala on behalf of their company. "I know you and Sophia mentioned you'll be too busy working the event to take an escort, but can I at least reserve a dance or two?"

"I would love it, Harrison. Thank you and Luke for your support. It means a lot."

"I'm sure I can wrangle up more interest. I've got calls out to a few of my associates."

"I really appreciate it." Ella is moved.

"Well, I've got to run—a client meeting. I'm looking forward to Saturday night," says Harrison, his voice lowering and becoming softer, which Ella finds exceptionally alluring.

"Me, too." Ella feels a sudden welcome chemical reaction as they say their goodbyes for now.

Full of nervous excitement after she chats with Harrison, Ella gets up from her desk and heads toward the office kitchen to make herself a cup of lemon citrus tea. While the water is getting ready to boil, she reaches into the cookie jar and pulls out an individually wrapped chocolate-orange biscotti.

"Must be the three o'clock hour," proclaims Sophia dramatically as she enters the kitchen. "Coffee and a snack are calling me too. Hey, what's that silly grin on your face?"

Ella chuckles. "You know me like a book. Harrison called."

"And?"

"He and Luke are purchasing a table of ten for the gala. That brings our total number of guests to three hundred and ten."

"Woo-hoo!" Sophia claps gleefully. "How are things between you and Luke by the way?"

After Sophia and Ella joined Harrison and Luke for a Beatles-cover-band concert, Sophia and Luke, both recovering from previous relationships—Sophia from her late husband's death followed by a brief relationship with a now-convicted romance scam artist, and Luke from a bad breakup from a toxic relationship—have since dated each other casually now and then but kept their togetherness as more of a friendship.

"I'm always happy to see Luke. But you know me, I'm happy in friendship mode for now. One day at a time."

"I thought so too, but then came Carter again, and now Harrison. One thing I know, the more I see and talk to Harrison, the more I like him but I'm taking it slow—and I'm really looking forward to our date Saturday."

Sophia smiles, happy for her friend. "So, Carter has some competition?"

Ella shrugs. "One day at a time." The ladies chuckle.

"Did you ask Carter if he'll perform at the gala?"

"Not yet. I will, though, when he takes me to dinner next Friday."

"Are you going to tell Harrison?"

"*Absolutely not.* That wouldn't be right. Besides, wasn't it you who recently told me, 'My motto is, until both parties agree to date exclusively, all is fair in love and war.' And as my grandmother always told me, 'Choose the one who treats you the best.' No need to rush. Time will tell."

"That's my girl," grins Sophia. The ladies clink their drinking mugs in a toast.

Later that afternoon, Ella receives more good news regarding the gala—Rosemary is working on a painting that she'll donate for the silent auction. Lester Sinclair, the gentleman who gifted Ella with the beautiful Christmas tree topper, and his wife, Penelope, will donate a week's stay at their luxurious Palm Beach, Florida, condominium, just one of Sinclair's many rental properties.

Moments later, Ella's cell phone chimes. "Hi, Sis. Any news about the boys who knocked over Rosemary's nativity set?"

"Turns out Adam, who is thirteen, and two of his seventh-grade buddies, prompted by the recent headline news and on a copycat dare, instigated one another to attack Rosemary's nativity set. None of the boys have records or have been involved in anything like this before, and from what we gathered, they're good students."

"Really?"

"Adam appears to have been the ringleader. His parents are going through a bitter divorce. So perhaps he's acting out."

"Could be. What's next?"

"Well, since there is no property damage and no one got physically assaulted, we'll take Rosemary up on her offer to speak to the boys. Putting a bit of a scare into them so they realize there are consequences to their actions will be a good learning experience."

"Wow. I want to be there when she talks to the boys."

"You'll have to talk to Rosemary about that. We're escorting the boys to her house tomorrow afternoon at four o'clock."

"Okay. What about the other culprits, the ones breaking windows and destroying holiday decorations at local retailers? And the guys who made off with the crates of wine from The Cottage Dining and Reading Room?"

"Those investigations are still in progress. However, those offenders won't get off as easy as Adam and his buddies."

"I'm sorry," bemoans Adam Black, a tall, skinny kid with braces, red hair, and freckles. Obviously ashamed, he is staring at his feet as he stands on Rosemary's porch. His other two buddies, Charlie Moses and Timmy Baird, who have already apologized, stand sullen at Adam's side.

"Come on in, boys." Rosemary ushers the boys and Julie, in her police uniform, into the great room, where Ella sits on the sofa nursing a cup of tea.

"Please, everyone, sit," directs Rosemary. "This is my neighbor, Ms. Ella Martin." Ella nods hello to the boys and Rosemary continues firmly, "What you did, boys, was very wrong." The boys look even more downtrodden as Rosemary asks, "What do you think your punishment should be?"

The boys, surprised to be asked this question, look at one another and then to Rosemary and shrug.

"Maybe help you out with some household chores?" offers Adam.

"I'm good at shoveling snow," suggests Charlie.

"Me, too," adds Timmy. "I go grocery shopping for my Ma. I could do that for you, ah, if you want." Timmy looks at his shoes again. "And I guess I could turn over my iPhone for a week."

Charlie and Adam shoot Timmy a stabbing look.

"What?" Timmy looks at Charlie and Adam and shrugs. "Got any better ideas?"

"Well, I was thinking of something quite different." Rosemary gets up and paces around the boys, who look like they are about to be sick. "Do you boys celebrate Christmas?"

"Yes." The boys nod their heads and answer in unison.

"Okay, then let's start with you, Adam. What is the meaning of Christmas?"

"Ah, I, uh, it's a holiday celebrated every December when Santa delivers toys."

The room is silent.

"And you, Charlie? What do you think Christmas means?"

"It's when we put up colorful decorations and family comes together to have a big meal and give presents."

"Timmy?"

"It's the one day of the year when my family goes to church."

"Oh, really?" Rosemary stares at the boys, which causes them to fidget nervously in their seats. "So, that's what Christmas is all about? Santa, the food, presents, and the one day of the year we go to church?"

Adam gulps, and the other two boys look at one another for answers. Ella bites her lip, trying not to laugh. Julie clears her throat to refrain from indicating her amusement. For a sweet older lady, Rosemary exudes authority, which makes the boys shake with fear as they wonder if their answers are correct, as well as the uncertainty about their intended "punishment."

"Have any of you boys ever read the Bible?" asks Rosemary.

The boys look perplexed and shake their heads.

"In the Bible, the Gospel of John Three, Sixteen, states, '*For God so loved the world: He gave His only Son, so that everyone who believes in Him may not perish but may have eternal life.*' Christmas is a celebration, an acknowledgment of this beautiful, transformative *act of love and mercy."*

The boys look sheepish. About to laugh out loud now, Ella coughs to regain control. Rosemary is telling it like it is.

"I'm going to give you boys an assignment. I want you to pick out a book or story focusing on Christmas. Read it, and then write an essay on the deeper meaning of Christmas. Explain how the Savior's birth was prophesized before it happened, the circumstances surrounding the Lord's birth, how it changed the world and humanity's salvation, and why we celebrate this blessed event and tradition. You can leave out the Santa references. Then I would like you to explain how your mistreatment of the manger does not represent Christ's teachings. Incorporate the Golden Rule, which explains how and why we should treat one another."

The boys cower, heads lowered.

"If it's okay with Officer Landon, I'll have the boys join me here at my house at four o'clock two weeks from today to read and discuss the essays. Does that work for you, Detective?"

Julie nods.

"Boys?"

The boys nod in agreement.

"Okay, gentlemen." Julie stands. "Let's leave Mrs. Engle and Miss Martin to their afternoon." The boys follow Julie out to the police car.

"You were brilliant, Rosemary," praises Ella. "An essay on the meaning of Christmas and a deep dive into how their actions go against the Lord's teaching. Brilliant!"

Rosemary chuckles. "They've got to learn. Their souls depend on it. I believe their misbehavior was a blessing in disguise."

Stronger Together

"Without a sense of caring, there can be no sense of community."

~~Anthony J. D'Angelo,
author, speaker, and business owner

Chapter Nine

The rest of Ella's week turns out to be much less dramatic than it was at the start. Now that it's Saturday morning, Ella takes the opportunity to sleep in for an extra hour before heading toward the kitchen to brew some coffee. She loves mornings like this when she has nothing special to do except enjoy a leisurely breakfast, scan the latest news on her computer or phone, pick up where she left off reading a favorite book, or pamper herself in whatever suits her desire.

The only absolute to-do on her list today is to get ready for her dinner date tonight with Harrison at six.

Sipping her coffee, Ella heads back toward her bedroom closet to pick out an outfit for this evening's dinner at The Water's Edge—a sophisticated, atmospheric venue. Romantic if she had to categorize it. After trying several possibilities, she chooses a classic, form-fitting black dress from her walk-in closet. The dress, exuding an air of elegance, is a perfect match for the sophisticated atmosphere of The Water's Edge. The black knit has long sleeves, a knee-length hemline, and black lace around the scoop neck. It will pair perfectly with black pumps, sheer stockings, pearl earrings, and a necklace.

As Ella heads back toward the kitchen to fix herself some breakfast, the doorbell rings. She tightens her robe and peeks through her front door's peephole. It's a flower delivery man. She opens the door.

"Hello, Miss," says the twenty-something delivery man wearing a jacket printed with the name "Danny" over the left breast pocket. Underneath the pocket reads: "Lavender Hill Cove Florists—Flower Delivery."

Danny hands Ella a large gift bag. Inside are two boxes. She pulls out a long black box. From the see-through window, she can see twelve, stunning, long-stem roses.

"Roses! They're gorgeous!" Ella places the gift bag on a table just inside her front door.

"The other box is the vase," states Danny.

"I wonder who sent them?" Ella sees a sealed envelope addressed with her name attached to the box.

"There's a gift card inside. If you could sign right here." Danny holds out a tablet and points to where Ella can sign electronically. With her right index finger, she squiggles her name on the signature line, which although illegible, confirms her receipt.

Ella immediately takes the box of roses to the kitchen, excited to see who sent the beauties. Placing the container on the counter, she rips open the accompanying envelope and reads:

Dear Ella,

I'm looking forward to our date next Friday. I want you to know that I'm thinking of you.

With love,

Carter

"Oh my," sighs Ella, surprised. She had thought the roses might be from Harrison. She removes a sizeable red vase from the box in the gift bag and fills it with water and the plant food accompanying the roses. Next, in the kitchen sink, she pulls the water tubes off each of the twelve long stems. With scissors, she cuts each rose stem on the diagonal and arranges the roses among the baby's breath and greens that came in the box. The result is a gorgeous display.

"This calls for another cup of coffee." Ella fills her mug, topping it off with some frothed almond milk and cinnamon as she ponders Carter's gift.

Could Carter have come to some realizations about how he's living his life regarding commitment?

While Carter's gift is thoughtful and beautiful, Ella still wonders about his motives and what he wants from her. Would Carter pursue her if she hadn't seen him that night for dinner with Sophia and Julie?

Their date next Friday will be interesting.

Looking at the roses and appreciating them for what they are—things of beauty—Ella decides not to dwell on the past or attempt to predict the future but, instead, to let things be, see things as they are, and not project her wishes or desires. To be courteous, she texts Carter a thank you, accompanied by a photo of the roses.

Carter immediately texts back:

> You're welcome. I'll be in touch soon. Have a good weekend. Love, Carter XO

Ella thinks about responding but realizes there is no need. She contemplates Carter's "XO." Years ago, and more recently when they connected after Jack's passing, Ella would have been ecstatic to receive roses and XOs from Carter. Hindsight is proving a valuable tool, however. Once or twice burned affects a person. In Ella's case, because of her tenacity and research to understand the meaning behind certain behaviors and personalities, combined with her life experience, she can look at a person or persons differently now. She has learned not to take what is said at face value and realizes that beautiful words, professions, and packaging do not mean a person has trustworthy or mutual intentions. Her belief in a higher power and adherence to traditional values and church teachings have also given her particular graces such as discernment, keen intuition, and a serene comfort, knowing she is spiritually protected following God's will and commandments. While life has its ups, downs, twists, and turns, she is confident she will never again have to fear giving her heart to someone who will break it. Her past pain has removed those rose-colored glasses without making her bitter, and for that, Ella is hugely grateful.

Moments later, her cell phone rings. It's Sophia, anxious to learn what transpired with Rosemary and the boys who knocked over the manger.

"Rosemary instructed the boys to write an essay on the meaning of Christmas and why their actions were not in line with the holiday spirit," Ella tells her.

"Brilliant!"

"That's just what I told Rosemary." Ella pauses. She's had a light bulb moment. "Hey, I just had a brainstorm."

"Those are usually awesome . . . so—"

"How about I call Doris—"

"Doris Banks from the library?"

"Yes. What if Firefly Lane Farm Events and Catering sponsors an essay contest working in conjunction with the Lavender Hill Cove Library? We could work with Doris, who would coordinate with the schools. Students would be instructed to write a short essay on the meaning of Christmas. We could involve elementary, middle school, and high school students and have winners from each school attend the gala with their families, where they'll be honored with a certificate or plaque and, maybe, an iPad and a cash scholarship."

"I love it," Sophia praises. "It ties in perfectly with our original mission for holding the gala—to support the library's new children's wing but can we mount a contest like that so quickly? And get companies to donate the iPads or funds for the cash awards?"

"I'll talk to Doris ASAP. She has contacts at the local schools on speed dial. I'll also contact the local paper and TV stations."

"And I'll contact more of our vendors about contributing to the scholarships. It's great media exposure for the sponsors and rich in community goodwill. Hey, maybe whoever sponsors the contest can serve on the judging panel."

"Great idea, Sophia. Of course, Doris will serve as a judge. I'd also like to ask Rosemary. After all, Rosemary's essay homework for Adam and his friends is the inspiration for the contest."

"So much for my relaxing Saturday."

"Ditto." Ella chuckles. "As soon as we get off the phone, I'm going to my desk to send out some emails and make a few calls."

"Me too. I like this idea, Ella. It's a great add to the cause and will make people think about the deeper meaning of Christmas, which, as we've discussed, is sometimes lost these days in all the commercialism and fanfare."

Hours later, Ella is pleased with the headway she's made. The Lavender Hill Cove librarian, Doris Banks, has agreed to contact the schools. One first-place scholarship will be presented to a lucky boy or girl in elementary school and middle school. And a third will be awarded to a fortunate high school student. In just a few short hours, Ella has also garnered an essay scholarship sponsor, Michael's Grocery Store, on board for $1,500, while Sophia has mange to land the Knights of Columbus for another $1,500. Now, there are only two more sponsored prizes to go. Ella glances at the time on her computer screen, which reads 4:00 p.m.

That's enough contest outreach for today.

Still in her PJs, Ella chooses to have plenty of time to bathe and dress before Harrison arrives.

"Wow! You look stunning," Harrison compliments, his voice filled with genuine admiration. He is dressed to impress in a stylish, slim-fitted charcoal gray wool herringbone coat and black pants, paired with a black turtleneck.

"You look great too. I like the black cowboy boots."

"Yeah, they make a fashion statement now, don't they?" His black cashmere turtleneck accentuates his sparkling blue eyes as he laughs. Then he presents Ella with a beautiful bouquet of red roses.

"Harrison!" gushes Ella, completely caught off guard. "They're beautiful." She lowers her head to take in the fragrant bouquet. "Ahh, what a fragrance—simply yummy."

"Beautiful flowers for a beautiful woman." That line from another man might sound a bit corny, but from Harrison, it's genuine.

"Let me put them in some water," remarks Ella, her face warm and flushed as she heads toward the kitchen. "Please, come join me."

Ella is thankful Carter's roses are tucked away in another room. It's not that Harrison would inquire as to who sent them, but Ella wouldn't want to have to discuss the sender *just in case.*

"I like what you've done with the place," notes Harrison, looking around the comfortable kitchen. Complimentary country- and beach-inspired paintings, objets d'art, and the white, dreamy teal, pale yellow, and sand tones converge to create a soothing ambiance. "You've been acquiring some unique art, I see."

Ella has transformed her home and kitchen since Harrison and his company installed her outdoor pergola some months ago, and she is pleased that Harrison appreciates her efforts. "I love antiquing," she admits as she cuts each rose stem on the diagonal to extend their life.

"And decorating. You've created a very welcoming atmosphere."

"Why, thank you." This comment, coming from Harrison, an architect/contractor/designer himself, is a compliment.

Ella picks out a white, hand-crafted ceramic vase from her kitchen cabinet, fills it with water and the packet of plant food from the flower's wrapping, and places the beautiful flowers at the center of her kitchen table. She admires the view and flashes Harrison a smile. "Perfect."

Moments later, Harrison and Ella leave for their dinner reservation at The Water's Edge.

"I love all the holiday lights," Ella says, marveling at the multicolored display against the dark, winter evening sky.

"Have you been to Santa Claus Lane yet?"

"No. Where is it?"

"After dinner, I'll take you there. It's a residential street where neighbors try to one-up each other with holiday decor. I hope those local vandals don't try anything on that street."

"Oh my. Speaking of vandals, my neighbor Rosemary and I saw three teens knocking over the holiday manger on Rosemary's front lawn. When we yelled at them to stop, they ran away."

"Was there a lot of damage?"

"The nativity statues were turned over, and hay was strewn about, but that was all. However, I found a wallet in the snow listing a name and address, which led Julie to investigate. Turns out it was a first-time offense for all three kids—a copycat situation emulating the vandals wreaking havoc on the local retail stores."

"What's the upshot with the teens?"

"Julie drove the boys in her police car to Rosemary's. The boys apologized, and Rosemary gave them a homework assignment. Each boy must write an essay on the meaning of Christmas and how their actions were out of line with the Christmas spirit."

Harrison nods approvingly. "Excellent! That will teach them a valuable lesson."

"Exactly. Rosemary's idea gave me the idea to organize an essay contest with the same theme. I'm coordinating with the local library and schools, and Sophia and I have even started to put together a panel of judges. We'll present three scholarships—one for elementary school, one for middle school, and one for high school at the Once Upon a Cove Christmas Gala. We've already got two fifteen-hundred-dollar donations."

"Grant and Sons can contribute the third."

"Really?"

"Of course, it would be our pleasure. It's a great cause. People have become desensitized to the meaning of Christmas. It's become so commercial."

"Thank you, Harrison. That's wonderful. Would you like to be on our panel of judges?"

"Count me in. I enjoy doing what I can for our community."

During dinner, after going over more details about the upcoming gala, Ella and Harrison discuss their childhood, the importance of family, and a bit about their previous dating histories. Harrison shares more details about the demise of his engagement that ended when he discovered his intended was cheating on him and leading a double life.

"Just like my brother, Justin," Ella shares.

"Would you like to be married again someday?" asks Harrison.

Ella is surprised by the question. Although they referred to their desires for the future at their recent lunch date, this question is more direct, and from her experience, men usually like to steer clear of any direct talk of marriage and commitment.

"Yes. I liked being married and having someone to love."

"I like that idea."

"I'm sorry it didn't work out for you with your ex-fiancé."

"I'm glad I found out what I did *before* we married. We professed that our values were the same, but obviously, they weren't. Cheating is a no-go in my book."

"My book too," agrees Ella. "I also would like it if my man would go to weekly mass with me. I think it's important to follow biblical teachings. When people don't, they become too invested in the world versus The Word."

"I'd like to accompany you to mass. I go to Sacred Heart. Where do you attend?"

"Sacred Heart."

"How come I haven't seen you? Saturday nights or on Sundays?"

"Usually Saturday, but we're out tonight, so I'll go tomorrow."

"Would you like to go together tomorrow?"

"I'd like that." Ella suddenly becomes emotional and feels like she wants to cry. She is wholly touched and surprised by Harrison.

Is he for real?

Ella tells herself to take a deep breath and not make a fool of herself. She reaches for her water glass, takes a sip, and then changes the subject, picking up on a topic they touched upon during their recent lunch date. "Harrison, you mentioned recently that you like to sail. How often do you take your boat out?"

For several minutes, while Harrison talks, Ella smiles and seemingly listens intently silently trying to assuage the scrambled thoughts screeching through her mind.

I could really go for Harrison.

Realizing that truth, Ella is petrified.

The Second Time Around?

"Life sometimes gives you a second chance."

~Maya Angelou

Ella promptly rises to the soft jazz emanating from her bedside clock-radio the following day. Groggy from little sleep after spending half the night reviewing the details of her date with Harrison, and pondering their church date today, she stumbles to the kitchen and pops a dark-roast coffee pod into her single-serve brew machine. Removing the container of almond milk from the fridge, she grabs another cup from the kitchen cabinet and froths half a cup of milk, which she pours into her mug after the coffee is brewed. She tops off the foam with a few sprinkles of cinnamon.

Next, she unplugs her cell phone from the kitchen counter charger, sits in the room's cozy nook, and scrolls through her texts as she sips her coffee. Her sister Julie's text invites Ella over for brunch after church. Ella responds:

> Sis. Harrison is going to church with me this morning. We may go out after. I know you'll say it's okay if I bring him. However, I'm unsure if I'm ready for him to meet the family. I'll call you later. Love, Me XO

While Ella looks forward to seeing Harrison this morning, she doesn't want to rush things. She reminds herself of the importance of going slow and getting to know who a person is by his actions, not just his words.

Church being at 9:00 a.m., Harrison will pick up Ella at 8:30, which gives her roughly a little over an hour to wash and dress. So, after answering the rest of her texts, including sending a thumbs up to Sophia for lining up three more judges for the essay contest, Ella consumes the remainder of her coffee and goes to take a shower.

For church, Ella opts for slim-fitting gray pants, made from a comfortable blend of cotton, polyester, and spandex, paired with black leather bootlets with a two-inch heel, and a plum-colored turtleneck. This ensemble, with its casual yet elegant charm, is further enhanced with silver hoop earrings and a matching, long, Y-shaped silver necklace with pearl adornments at the end. The outfit is completed with a single-breasted, three-quarter-length, black wool coat, ensuring both style and comfort.

Some twenty minutes later, Ella's doorbell rings.

"Good morning." Harrison greets her with a smile.

Ella notes how handsome Harrison looks in his charcoal-gray corduroy pants, navy wool coat, white turtleneck, and a reprise of his black cowboy boots. She appreciates a man who cares about his appearance, and today, Harrison certainly makes a statement with his "courting" attire.

"The air's quite nippy. I left the car running with the heat on." Harrison tells Ella.

"Let me grab my coat and bag, and we can be on our way."

During mass, Ella feels a soothing peace wash over her. It feels good to have a man by her side. Her husband, Jack, never wanted to attend mass; although he said he believed in a higher power, he wasn't interested in observing rites. Jack didn't have Ella's faith or her values. Several times throughout the liturgy, Harrison tenderly smiles at Ella, and she can't help but think he is a gentleman and attentive to her needs. He makes her feel special and protected. So far, his words and actions have demonstrated he is a well-adjusted, mature, and Godly man who can genuinely express himself. He feels good to Ella.

Stay calm, go slow, and don't overthink.

"I want to hear all the details," instructs Sophia the following day at work as she and Ella sip coffee in the Firefly Lane Farm Catering and Events conference room during their usual Monday afternoon brainstorming session.

Ella fills Sophia in on her Saturday dinner and Sunday church date with Harrison. "He's something else," she gushes.

"So when do you see him again?"

"This Saturday."

"So, Carter Friday and Harrison Saturday." Sophia chuckles. "You've got quite the dance card."

"I'm taking things very slow—not rushing into anything or building up unrealistic fantasies in my head."

"Well, Harrison and Carter both make for great fantasy material." The ladies break out in laughter.

"Let's behave now," Ella says playfully.

"If you insist," Sophia agrees as she opens her work binder. "Okay. There are some new gala updates to report. We currently have six judges and three money scholarships—from Knights of Columbus, Michael's Grocery, and Grant and Sons—all for fifteen hundred dollars each."

"Excellent." Ella opens her notebook to share her latest donor and school outreach with Sophia. "Green's Electronics emailed me this morning." She pauses to take a sip of her coffee. "They're also on board to donate three iPads—one for each winner."

"Woo-hoo!" Sophia claps jubilantly.

"However, we need *four* scholarships and *four* tablets."

"Oh?"

"Doris from the library called earlier," continues Ella. "She suggested we do four scholarships. The fourth one is for kindergarten through second grade, since those students are too young to write full-blown essays, but they can do a picture and a sentence or two. However, grades three through five will write essays, along with the middle and high school students."

"Works for me."

"I thought so, too. Let me tell you, Doris moves quickly. She already has a green light from the elementary, middle, and high school principals. So, if you want, I'll write up a draft press release that we can review before contacting the local media regarding news coverage."

"That sounds great. We just need to secure one more fifteen-hundred-dollar scholarship." Sophia gives Ella a thumbs-up and continues to review her notes. "Oh, Frank had a brilliant idea. Instead of the usual chiffon trifle, he suggested we go for something even more indulgent for dessert—individual chocolate mousse parfaits with a burst of fresh berries. What do you think?"

Frank Ross is Sophia and Ella's go-to head chef for extra-large events, and he always dreams up the most delicious ideas.

"You know me and chocolate."

"Me too. I just wanted to be sure. I'll tell Frank that chocolate mousse parfait it is!"

"I'm so glad we hired Frank and his crew. I love it when you and I cater small events but several hundred people? It's not really my thing."

"Ditto. Frank's a blessing. Everything he whips up is pure heaven."

Sophia and Ella review the final entrée selections. For starters, wait staff will serve guests a mixed-lettuce salad with cucumber, red onion, and olives, tossed in a champagne vinaigrette dressing with Parmesan crostini, followed by a dinner entrée of their choice—grilled salmon with a citrus glaze over a bed of julienne vegetables and herbed fingerling potatoes, succulent filet mignon with the same vegetable and potato sides, or a vegetarian linguine pasta made with mushrooms and spinach in a tomato-herb sauce. And now, for the meal's divine ending, chocolate mousse parfait with berries.

"Have you heard back from the band?" asks Ella.

"The Seagulls' manager emailed me this morning and offered us a great deal—twenty-five-hundred dollars."

"Wow! That's half their usual rate!"

"They also asked to be mentioned in any press releases and the evening's program—good publicity for them."

"I'm okay with that."

"And more good news—in addition to performing during the meal, they'll also arrange for a piano player and singer for the cocktail hour," Sophia exclaims. "Things couldn't be going better. Do you still want to ask Carter about playing as our headliner?"

Ella nods. "Yes. Carter's a definite draw and we need to sell more tickets. It's probably best to ask him in person so, so I'll ask when I see him for dinner."

The week roars along at high speed as Sophia and Ella continue taking care of various gala organizational details. On Friday, Ella leaves the Firefly Lane Farm Catering and Events offices early to prepare for her date that evening with Carter.

After showering, careful not to disturb yesterday's color, cut, and blow-out, Ella expertly applies her makeup, and after trying on a pretty, red, V-necked cocktail dress, which she deems is "too sexy," she decides to opt for a more sophisticated and elegant alternative, a knee-length, long-sleeved, forest green dress that she pairs with black boots and a stunning, long silver necklace with an oversized, polished red jasper teardrop stone and matching earrings.

As she gets ready, Ella wonders how the dinner conversation with Carter might go. Before she contemplates various possibilities, she stops herself.

Take it moment by moment, Ella. No expectations. Listen to what Carter has to say.

In fact, not to get ahead of herself—or Carter, for that matter—she is meeting him at the Sandpiper restaurant, just in case things go south or she needs a quick getaway.

The Sandpiper parking lot is full as Ella drives onto the lot. After all, it's the holiday season, and the Sandpiper, a Zagat-rated venue, is a local and visitor favorite.

"Thank you, Lord," murmurs Ella as she scores a parking spot near the restaurant's entrance. She quickly surveys her appearance in the car visor's mirror. Makeup and hair all in place, she takes a deep, cleansing breath for fortification before exiting her vehicle.

After she checks her black leather jacket with the coat check, she walks to the hostess's table. "Carter Huxley's table, please."

The restaurant, beautifully appointed for the holiday season, is a comfortable and romantic setting decorated in natural woods and furnishings in shades of white and beige hues, which pair perfectly with the water views and beachside setting. The soft white lights decorating the venue create a cozy and intimate feel.

"Right this way, Miss," answers the pretty, twenty-something hostess. The young woman's black dress slacks and a long-sleeve white silk blouse exude a classy charm befitting the restaurant's upscale image.

"You look amazing, Ella," Carter compliments as Ella approaches the window-view table. He stands and pulls out a chair next to his. As Ella sits, the hostess places a menu at each of the two place settings.

A waiter immediately approaches the table. "Something to drink, Miss?"

Ella looks at Carter's setting and notices he's drinking red wine.

"I'm having a cab," he says. "But please, order whatever you prefer."

"Chardonnay, please." Ella turns to Carter. "How did your session go this past week?"

"Smoothly, thank goodness."

"When will your album be for sale?"

Carter beams. "Next spring."

"I'm looking forward to hearing it."

The waiter sets down Ella's glass of wine. "Would you like to order now?"

"Give us about ten more minutes, Brian," answers Carter before turning his attention back to Ella. "If you'd like, I can play some tracks for you."

"I'd like that, and speaking of playing some music tracks, do you mind if we get a little business out of the way?"

"Sure." Carter looks intrigued.

"Remember a while back you mentioned you'd love to play at one of the Firefly Lane Farm events that benefit a local charity?"

Carter nods.

"Well, we're hosting a gala at the Farm to contribute funds to support the construction of a new children's wing at the Lavender Hill Cove library. We're also coordinating a special Christmas essay scholarship contest with the library and local schools, and as of today, we've sold just over three hundred tickets, and the venue can hold four hundred. There'll be a performance by The Seagulls, and DJ Cory Michaels will serve as our MC and—"

"And you want me to play?"

"Oh, Carter, it would mean so much. It would be great if you would be our headliner and play for maybe thirty minutes or so—or however long you're willing to play."

"What's the budget?" asks Carter, deadpan.

"Ah, um, ah." Ella is flustered. Their budget would definitely not accommodate a professional like Carter.

"Kidding," Carter says in a sing-song voice. "It's a charity event for the community. I'm in, free of charge!"

"Carter, you don't know how much this means. Would you mind it if we use your name in media releases?"

"You're quite the negotiator," Carter replies with a laugh. "Of course. I like the idea, and the fact it's tied in with the library and schools. What type of scholarships are being presented?"

"Grades K through two will be submitting a painting to be judged, and elementary grades three through five, as well as middle school and high school students will all be submitting essays on the deeper meaning of Christmas—something sorely needed as many folks have forgotten why we celebrate the holiday. Each of the four winners will receive a fifteen-hundred-dollar scholarship."

"Who are the scholarship donors?"

"The Knights of Columbus, Michael's Grocery Store, and Grant and Sons. We need to secure one more fifteen-hundred-dollar scholarship. Oh, and Greens Electronics is donating four iPads."

"You mentioned Grant and Sons is donating. *Harrison Grant?*"

Ella clears her throat. "Yes."

"I know Harrison."

"You do?"

"Two years ago, he remodeled my house."

"Oh." Ella doesn't know what else to say. Frankly, she's a little unnerved that the two men know each other. She takes a sip of her chardonnay.

"Count me in for the fourth scholarship," says Carter.

Shocked, Ella almost spits out her drink. *"Really?"*

"Really," says Carter, smiling.

"Okay." Ella reminds herself to breathe and takes a deep breath.

Take things slowly. Let them unfold according to God's plan. But, God, precisely what is your plan?

Ella is amused at how events are unfolding. "Carter, you're being extremely generous. I don't want to pressure you or make you feel beholden, I—"

"Ella, I want to do this. Lavender Hill Cove is my home, and I love it. It's an honor to be able to contribute. And besides, anything for a friend."

Friend. *Friend.* There's that word again. The word that broke them up so many months ago when Ella, dating Carter exclusively at the time, thought they were on the same page but only because Carter led her to believe they were and that they had a future. However, when it came right down to it, when pressed in a situation that came up unexpectedly, Carter couldn't or wouldn't refer to Ella as his girlfriend, only as his *friend.* He then confessed to Ella that he was "a loner, a solitary soul, always moving on."

This new revelation indicated, without a doubt, that he and Ella were definitely *not* on the same page. Heartbroken and bruised, Ella held on to her self-respect and stood her ground. Carter's approach, promises, and words, she realized, were hot air. He wasn't what he professed.

Is he any different now?

"Yes, we are friends, aren't we?" After months of recuperating from the shock and status as "single again," Ella and Carter remained friendly and courteous when they accidentally ran into one another. Carter even wished her Happy Birthday and checked in occasionally. Ella was always cordial, never responded harshly or off-putting, being too much of a lady to do otherwise. While she let him know of her disappointment with his non-commitment, she proceeded with grace.

Ella's fingers smooth out a crease on the white tablecloth, and to her surprise, Carter places his hand over hers and squeezes.

"Ella, I know I upset you the last time we had dinner. I told you I was a loner and that I liked it that way. I'm so sorry I hurt you."

It would have been nice if I had known that up front.

"I was a jerk."

Ella perks up and waits for Carter to continue.

"I've thought a lot about my life, how I've lived, and especially about my actions and words. Truth be told, I think I said what I did because I was scared."

"Scared?"

"Of getting too close. Of letting someone—*you*—in."

"And things are different for you now?"

"I do want to share my life with one woman. I'm more conscious."

"What caused the change?"

"After we went our separate ways, I had a lot of time to think and observe friends and family who were happy in their relationships. I realized—and several of them pointed out—that I've had some shallow relationships. I've been a runner. However, what made me take a look at my life the most was spending time with one of my best buddies, Jackson."

"How so?"

"Jackson passed from cancer two months ago, leaving a wife and young son. He was only forty-six."

"I'm sorry."

"We talked almost every day about everything. Suddenly, Jackson's sickness, watching him with his family, and then going through the loss of a good friend, made me realize how fragile life is. It highlighted what's important . . . and what I didn't have."

Ella nods in understanding.

"I'm thrilled you said yes to joining me tonight. It's really good to see you."

"Well, thank you for asking."

A moment of silence between Ella and Carter is broken when the waiter, Brian, returns to take their dinner orders.

During dinner, Carter and Ella catch up on their lives and talk about their families and town happenings.

"I'd like to get together again soon if you're willing," says Carter as he walks Ella to her car.

Ella waits to respond as she thinks about what accepting Carter's offer might mean. "If I agree to see you, we'd have to start at ground zero. I've changed too, Carter. I've been living my life and taking things slow across the board."

Carter nods.

"Let's talk in a few days," Ella says softly, not wanting to commit to anything without sufficient time to mull it over.

"I'll call you. In the meantime, I'll have my manager, Billy, reach out regarding the scholarship and any PR material you may need to help promote the gala."

"Thank you."

Carter leans in to kiss Ella. She lets him kiss her briefly, but his mesmerizing lips and scent, his stunning looks, beautiful eyes, and charming way with words don't have quite the same effect as in the past. This time, rather than letting herself get swept away, she proceeds with caution, allowing things to unfold one step at a time.

The Deeper Meaning of Christmas

"What if Christmas he thought, doesn't come from a store. What if Christmas . . . perhaps . . . means a little bit more."

~Dr. Seuss,
How the Grinch Stole Christmas!

Chapter Eleven

The media response to the essay contest is overwhelming. Not only does The Lavender Hill Cove Courier print a front-page news article, but Ella and Sophia are interviewed twice on the six o'clock evening news, along with the headline entertainer, Carter Huxley. The exposure immediately boosts ticket sales, resulting in a sold-out event, and there is even a three-page waiting list for cancellations.

"Maybe we should have charged more for tickets," Sophia remarks as she and Ella sip their afternoon tea and review the gala updates.

"Next year," replies Ella with a sparkle in her eye.

Sophia nods. "So, are you going to go out with him again?"

"Carter or Harrison?"

"Oh, you sly devil, you."

Ella laughs. "I've been taking it slow to see who's a go or no-go."

"That's my girl."

"What about you? Don't you want to get back in the saddle again?"

"Maybe. But not until after the gala. Too much yet to do. We'll see what the new year and the good Lord brings."

"My sentiments, exactly."

Ella and Sophia share a smile. Sophia is still healing, thinks Ella. She's right to take it slow like me.

Sophia was married to Harold, a wonderful man who was an excellent match for her. They shared many happy years. Working and farming at Firefly Lane Farm was their dream come true until Harold received a fatal cancer diagnosis and passed away. After two years of mourning, Sophia finally started dating again and met an extremely handsome and charismatic man, Jesse Hayes, on an online dating site. Just about then, Ella decided to remain in her childhood hometown of Lavender Hill Cove following her husband Jack's passing.

One fateful day, while enjoying antique shopping and lunch with a water view, Ella and Julie spotted Jesse and another woman in a romantic embrace. Worried for Sophia's emotional well-being upon finding out her romantic partner was a cheater, the sisters began their private investigation, which turned up some shocking revelations—not only was Jesse a serial cheater, but he also had a lurid history of scamming many unsuspecting widows out of their fortunes. Luckily for Sophia, Julie and Ella were able to expose Jesse's intentions before Sophia suffered too much damage, but not before a harrowing kidnapping experience.

His misdeeds discovered, Jesse kidnapped Ella and Sophia, absconding to one of his paramours' cabins in the hopes of securing a secret getaway. However, Julie, being a relentless detective, assembled the mystery pieces, locating and freeing Ella and Sophia. Eventually, by a sheer twist of Divine Fate, Ella and Julie captured Jesse before he gathered more victims into his deceitful web.

Ella, forever believing that Sophia deserves the best, is relieved when Sophia expresses her willingness to consider dating in the new year. Sophia's reply is a hopeful sign, as many in Sophia's situation would have closed their hearts to future relationships.

On her drive home later that afternoon, Ella's stomach rumbles as she ponders dinner. Suddenly remembering that due to her busy work schedule and appointments, her fridge needs restocking, she takes the opportunity of a free night to grocery shop.

Once parked and inside the market, she slowly peruses the isles, depositing needed items in her basket.

"Well, hello, Ella!" Rosemary greets Ella. She is accompanied by Adam, Charlie, and Timmy, the boys who almost destroyed her Christmas manger display. "Boys, you remember my neighbor, Ella Martin."

"Yes," reply the boys with sheepish grins.

"The boys are helping me shop, and then we're going to make homemade pizza and salad for dinner."

"Really?" says Ella, surprised.

"The boys have been very, very helpful around my house, haven't you boys?"

"We helped Miss Rosemary organize her bookshelves," responds Adam proudly.

"We helped vacuum and clean her house," Charlie offers.

"And chopped wood for her fireplace," chimes in Timmy. "My father helped too."

"Well, I'm impressed." Ella grins.

Rosemary is amazing—an angel, actually.

"The boys have even come to my house after school—"

"We play word games, and Miss Rosemary bakes us peanut butter cookies—"

"And we have apple-cinnamon squares!" Timmy declares with enthusiasm. "Sometimes we even watch movies."

Ella takes a deep breath, not quite knowing what to make of this newly formed circle of unusual friends.

"Would you like to join us for pizza and salad tonight?" offers Rosemary. "The boys are going to read me their essays."

"Oh, now that is an offer I can't refuse. How about I bring dessert? Maybe brownies and ice cream?"

The boy's faces light up.

"Wonderful. Come over at six thirty." Rosemary smiles warmly.

"Perfect. See you all soon," Ella says as she pushes her cart toward the next aisle, marveling at this chance meeting. She intended to ask Rosemary if she could hear the boys read their essays.

Upon arriving home, and after putting all her groceries away in their proper places, Ella quickly changes into a more comfortable outfit—black leggings and a comfy, long, blue cowl neck sweater paired with her tan ankle boots lined with faux fur.

In the kitchen, she removes the three-pint container of vanilla fudge ice cream from the freezer, places it in her canvas shopping tote, along with the store-bought brownies, and heads toward Rosemary's.

"The pizzas are almost ready," announces Adam gleefully to Ella as he answers Rosemary's front door.

"I can smell them baking. The aroma is fantastic." Ella sniffs, breathing in deeply. "I brought brownies and ice cream." She holds up the tote to Rosemary as she enters the kitchen.

"The boys will love having brownies and ice cream for dessert," Rosemary says and, taking the bag from Ella, deposits the brownies onto the kitchen counter and the ice cream in the freezer.

"What type of pizza are we having?" Ella asks.

"We cut up meatballs, onions, mushrooms, and there's all kinds of cheeses on top," reports Timmy.

Ella sniffs appreciatively. "The pizza sauce smells divine."

"My recipe. I made it over the weekend," replies Rosemary.

"Can I help with anything?"

"Everything will be ready in about five minutes." Rosemary peeks at the creation through the oven's glass. "The table's set, and the salad—minus the dressing—is in the fridge. Let's have a few appetizers before we eat. Charlie, would you be a dear and take the cheese, crackers, guacamole, and chips into the living room?"

"Sure."

"Ella, can I get you a glass of wine? A cabernet or chardonnay?" asks Rosemary.

"Cab' for me." Ella grabs a blue corn chip as Charlie walks past her with the appetizer tray.

"Rosemary, how did you do it?"

"What?"

"The boys. Looks like you all have become best buds. How did it all happen?"

"Well, I got a few calls asking about writing the essays, and one thing led to another. I mentioned that I needed help with this and that, and the boys were only too happy to offer assistance. We've had so much fun in the process and getting to know one another."

"I'm astounded and extremely impressed."

Rosemary winks. "Come, the boys will wonder what's happened to us."

After appetizers and chitchat, the boys sit at the dining table while Ella and Rosemary serve the pizzas and Caesar salad.

"Yum. This pizza's the best I've ever had," cries Adam, chewing.

"Yeah," Charlie agrees, taking a mammoth bite and then gulping it down with soda.

"You boys were a big help tonight and, in fact, all week," praises Rosemary before biting into a forkful of salad.

The boys, who had sour faces and were considered unruly several weeks before, have done a complete one-eighty. Ella smiles, impressed with their transformation. Perhaps all they needed was a little supervision and loving attention. Rosemary has obviously made them feel welcome and special. She definitely has a way with children—and adults, too, for that matter.

"Boys, what do you think? Read your essays and then have dessert?"

The boys nod, all in agreement.

Rosemary and Ella sit on one side of Rosemary's comfortable sofa. After the boys decide Adam will go first, Timmy and Charlie settle in on the sectional opposite the ladies.

"I picked "A Christmas Carol," by Charles Dickens," begins Adam. "It's a novella."

"What's a novella?" blurts out Timmy.

"It's shorter than a novel but longer than a short story," Adam answers proudly.

"Very good, Adam," Rosemary acknowledges. "That's correct."

"'A Christmas Carol' begins with the miserly Ebenezer Scrooge.

He's a mean, elderly British man who lends money to people and charges high interest rates. He's grumpy to everyone: his employee Bob Cratchit, the community, and even his family. However, one Christmas Eve, he's visited by his deceased business partner, Jacob Marley, who comes to warn Mr. Scrooge to change his ways.

"Jacob is in chains, and his message is to let Scrooge know he has a single chance of redemption if he wants to avoid the same fate. He tells Scrooge he will be visited by three spirits—Christmas Past, Present, and Yet to Come." Adam continues to relay details about the story.

"Very good," praises Rosemary and Ella nods in agreement. "Why do you think it was important that these three spirits visited Scrooge?" Rosemary prompts.

"When the ghost of Christmas Past visits Scrooge, Scrooge gets to see how he had a much nicer nature as a young man with his cheerful boss, Fezziwig. Then, Scrooge, allowing his love of money to take over his life, loses love because his fiancée claims Scrooge loves money more than he loves her. Scrooge learns how his love of money took first place in his life, costing him love and other opportunities."

"What does he learn from the other ghosts?" asks Rosemary.

"The Ghost of Christmas Present shows Scrooge a happy Christmas scene in his employee Bob Cratchit's home. Scrooge becomes sad when he sees the weak but good-natured Tiny Tim, and when the ghost takes Scrooge to his nephew's home, we see how his nephew and friends joke that Scrooge is a 'ridiculous fellow.'"

"Then the Ghost of Christmas Future shows Scrooge that he will have a fate even more horrible afterlife than Jacob Marley."

"How?" asks Rosemary.

"The Ghost scares Scrooge when he shows him a grave with his name on it, Scrooge's dead body underneath bedsheets, and a scene where people are selling Scrooge's worldly goods without remorse or sadness for him. And finally, he shows how Scrooge's ill and miserly treatment toward Bob Cratchit will result in the death of Tiny Tim."

"What does Scrooge learn in the end?"

"He learns how his cruel and uncaring attitude negatively affected and influenced lives. He gets insight into his motivations. Seeing all this, and not wanting to end up like Marley, motivates Scrooge to become more conscious and kinder."

"Excellent, Adam. Very well done," compliments Rosemary, and Adam beams. "Timmy, you're up."

"I chose a short story by O. Henry," begins Timmy. "It's called 'The Gift of the Magi.' Jim and Della are a newly married couple. They love each other a lot and are devoted to one another. It's almost Christmas, and they both wonder what to give one another. They don't have much money, but they each want to give the other something that will bring the other great joy. Della has gorgeous long hair that reaches past her knees, and Jim has a pocket watch that he treasures, which was handed down to him from his grandfather and father. To pay for a gold chain for Jim's pocket watch as a gift, Della cuts her lovely hair and sells it. And Jim sells his pocket watch so he can buy the combs that Della has admired for her hair."

"Why do you think Della and Jim sacrificed the things that meant the most to them?"

"Because of their love for one another. They were both willing to sacrifice—Della her hair, and Jim the family watch—to give the other person joy."

"Why do you think the story is named 'The Gift of the Magi'?"

"Oh, oh, I know!" Charlie shouts.

"Go ahead," encourages Rosemary.

"Wise men traveled to bring Jesus gifts at his birth in a manger."

"Right," Rosemary replies.

"And the Magi, wise kings and men," continues Charlie, "traveled far and wide to Jesus's birthplace to present him with gold as a symbol of kingship on earth, frankincense—which is an incense—as a sign of deity, and an embalming oil called myrrh, a symbol of one who is mortal. So, God and man together. Additionally, the three kings put themselves in terrible danger with the wicked King Herod, so much so that they changed their routes home to avoid Herod's summons."

"Very good, Charlie," Rosemary says. "Now, Timmy, let's get back to you. "You mentioned that in 'The Gift of the Magi,' both Della and Jim sacrificed the things that meant the most to them because of their love for one another. Were there any other messages?"

"Both Della's and Jim's sacrifices rendered their gifts to one another useless. So, another message is that love sometimes requires sacrifice and putting one's own needs and desires second. Love and selflessness—are truly the greatest gifts we can give." Timmy finishes proudly.

"Loving and caring for one another is the greatest gift," adds Ella.

"Precisely." Rosemary nods. "Excellent, Timmy. Excellent. It's your turn now, Charlie."

"I picked 'The Little Match Girl,' by Hans Christian Andersen. A young, homeless girl is sent out in the cold, snowy weather to sell matches to make money for her family. However, she doesn't have warm clothes because her family is poor. She starts to light the matches she's to sell to warm herself, and as she does, the girl sees comforting visions—a warm stove, a goose roasting, a beautiful Christmas tree. When the girl sees a vision of her dead grandmother, who loved and treated her better than anyone else, the girl, to keep her grandmother's vision before her, lights the entire bundle of matches. While she's freezing, she knows she can't go home without having made a sale or she'll face her father's anger, so the little match girl winds up freezing to death in the cold weather with her grandmother carrying her soul to heaven. It's a sad story."

"It is an *unfortunate* story. Why doesn't the little match girl have a name?" asks Rosemary.

"Maybe she represents all poor people?" Charlie answers.

"Good. Perceptive," praises Rosemary. "Why do you think Hans Christian Andersen wrote such a sad story? And what do you think the story represents?"

"Well, the matches give the girl warmth, and the visions she sees are nice—" Charlie begins.

"The visions represent hope. However, did anyone, seeing a poorly dressed little girl in the cold, stop to help?"

Charlie shakes his head no.

"Why? What do you think that means in the story?"

Charlie ponders this. "That we should help those in need. That it's mean not to help."

"Yes." Rosemary nods. "The author underscores the need to behave charitably toward those less fortunate. Do you boys know what the Bible says about how we should treat the poor?"

The boys look at one another and shrug.

Rosemary picks up her Bible sitting on a nearby hutch and navigates to Proverbs 19:17. She reads: "Whoever cares for the poor lends to the Lord who will pay back the sum in full." Next, she reads Proverbs 22:9. "The generous will be blessed, for they share their food with the poor." She then adds, "In the Gospel of Matthew, Jesus says, 'Come, you who are blessed by my Father. Inherit the kingdom prepared for you from the foundation of the world. For I was hungry and you gave me food, I was thirsty, and you gave me drink, a stranger and you welcomed me, naked and you clothed me, ill and you cared for me, in prison and you visited me.'"

"And what does Jesus say about how we should treat one another?" asks Rosemary.

"Oh, oh, I know this," Timmy yells. "Do unto others what you would have them do unto you."

"Correct! Do you boys know why Jesus was born?" asks Rosemary.

"To teach people things?" Charlie responds.

"Yes, but why was it so important that God sent his only son?"

The boys stare wide-eyed.

"Ella, care to share with the boys why?"

"Because of humankind's sin—disobeying God's commandments and laws of how we should live. Jesus was born to pay our debt. He was born for our salvation so that we might choose him and thus, in death, we may live forever eternally in Heaven with the Father."

Rosemary nods. "God is so holy that His eyes are too pure to look upon wickedness. He cannot endure the sight of evil, says the Bible. However, as God is abundantly good and merciful, he is also just. So, when we sin, if we wish to spend eternity with God versus the other place, we must atone and ask God for forgiveness. Jesus paid the debt to humanity after the fall of Adam and Eve. We can choose to follow His teachings and God's commandments or not."

"We have free will," adds Ella.

"However, before we choose, it's essential to think about the consequences of our actions," continues Rosemary. "And if we sin, we must ask for forgiveness, be sincerely repentant, and try not to make the same mistake again."

The boys look solemn for a few minutes, trying to absorb everything Rosemary has told them. Then Adam softly offers, "We're sorry we messed up your Christmas manger."

"Yeah," agree Charlie and Timmy.

"Your apology means a lot to me, and I forgive you." Rosemary smiles warmly.

"You boys did a wonderful job explaining the stories you read," compliments Ella. "They're important classic stories, and we can all benefit by remembering their messages."

"We probably wouldn't have read them if Miss Rosemary hadn't assigned them," Timmy scrunches up his nose in thought. "Is this what's called something good coming out of something bad?"

"Yes, Timmy. I believe so," Rosemary says. "And in a strange way, besides learning a few things, I'm very grateful I got to know you boys. I've appreciated all your help these past few weeks."

"We're happy to know you too, Miss Rosemary," Adam blurts out and the other boys nod their heads in agreement.

"Do you think we can do another movie night soon?" asks Adam.

"Of course." Rosemary beams. "Now, I don't know about you all, but my sweet tooth is calling. Is anyone interested in brownies and ice cream?

"Yeah!" The boys reply enthusiastically as Rosemary and Ella head toward the kitchen.

Coming Together in Celebration

"It is Christmas every time you let God love others through you."

~St. Teresa of Calcutta

Chapter Twelve

"The room looks amazing if I say so myself," Ella boasts as she and Sophia finish decorating the barn hall a day before the Once Upon a Cove Christmas Gala.

The hall is filled with round tables, each outfitted with white tablecloths, red napkins, and white china settings for ten people.

"These centerpieces work perfectly, too," Sophia says admiringly as she places a silver platter decorated with three-tiered, flameless white pillar candles surrounded by faux greenery and white and gold ornaments. "I'm glad we decided on making them ourselves. I think they work better than flowers."

"Agreed. They'll provide festive ambient light, and on the practical side, we can use the elements for future events," states Ella as she looks around the room. Strings of white lights surround the hall, at the end of which is a stunning, tall, artificial blue spruce decorated with sparkling white lights and gold, silver, white, and glass ornaments.

"Did you talk with Chef Frank about when his crew will arrive tomorrow?" asks Sophia.

"Oh, they'll be here bright and early. Six o'clock. I'll be here to let them in."

"Bless you for being an early riser." Sophia chuckles as she follows a seating chart and places table numbers on each table.

"Oh, I forgot to tell you," Ella adds. "Thanks to my neighbor Rosemary, we have three more volunteers to help us out tomorrow."

"Oh?"

"The boys who attempted to destroy her holiday manger. They've been successfully rehabilitated and happily volunteered to assist tomorrow."

"Great! The more help, the better. What shall we have them do?"

"I'm meeting them here at five o'clock to let them see the lay of the land. I figured one could help outside, guiding folks where to park, another with check-ins, and one on standby for whatever we need. I picked up a few more walkie-talkies so we can easily keep in touch."

"Works for me." Sophia looks over her to-do list as Ella checks out the decorations on the stage where the DJ will play dance music and Carter Huxley will entertain.

"Lookin' good up here too. All clean and spiffy," says Ella, admiring the manger setup with Mary, Joseph, and baby Jesus on one end and beautifully decorated trees at the opposite end of the stage.

"Say, did you get the technical guy to project the image of the old-fashioned street scene on the back of the stage?" Sophia asks.

"He'll be here later today to set up. It will look fantastic—a Dicken's holiday street scene."

"I love it . . . especially your idea of having the Dickens Carolers greet our guests as they arrive."

"We'll give everyone an experience to remember," Ella says as she checks her writing pad for additional to-do items.

"I'm headed back to my desk." Sophia walks toward the barn offices. "I have a few more calls and updates to make on the reservation list and seating arrangements. I'm also putting the scholarship winners at the tables up front closest to the stage so they can easily navigate to pick up their awards."

The award submission process, coordinated online at the Firefly Lane Farm Catering and Events website, had worked like a charm. Ella, Sophia, Doris from the library, and several other community representatives were able to divide and conquer the submissions, choosing four scholarship winners: two winners from elementary school—one from grades K-2 and one from grades 3-5—and a winner from both middle school and high school.

"I have a few more things to check, and then I'll be back in my office." Ella's cell phone rings, and when Harrison's name pops up on her caller ID, she feels a bolt of happy energy.

"How's the party planning coming along?" Harrison asks.

"Everything's in place. Just a few more minor details to tend to."

"Do you think you'll be able to take time to enjoy the gala?"

"I'm going to try." Ella chuckles. "You never know what will happen at one of these events, but I'll be on a walkie-talkie with Sophia to ensure everything goes as smoothly as possible."

"Well, I'm looking forward to it. Please let me know if I can help in any way."

"I think we have everything covered, but I'll let you know. You've already helped so much by providing a scholarship to one of the essay winners."

"Till tomorrow then."

"Till tomorrow. Bye." As she disconnects from the call, she is caught up in a sweet reverie for a moment or two. She can see Harrison's handsome face and warm smile in her mind. Then suddenly, she thinks of Carter. While she is still a free agent—not committed to dating any one man exclusively—up until this point she hasn't given much thought to the fact that both Harrison and Carter will be attending the gala.

Ella quickly reviews the scenario.

Harrison will sit at his table with his brother, Luke, and other people from Grant and Sons. Carter won't be attending, just performing. It may not even be an issue.

Ella pushes any negative thoughts out of her mind and thinks strictly of business. Harrison and Carter are community supporters, each contributing a scholarship to a student winner. She'll cross any awkward bridge when she gets to it.

Adam, Timmy, and Charlie meet Ella at the barn at five o'clock, and she shows them the lay of the land. At the same time, they discuss their positions for the event—Charlie will assist with directing the outside parking, Timmy will help work the guest check-in table, and Adam will serve as the floater.

"These walkie-talkies are cool." Timmy grins and speaks into the unit with a deep voice, "Come in, Adam. Do you read?"

"Adam, here. Yes, I read."

"How goes it?"

"Fine. But the fly on your pants is undone. Do you copy?"

Timmy's face turns beet red as he turns around and zips up his fly. The boys laugh and rag on Timmy.

Ella chuckles at the boys' banter. "Okay, boys. I need you to act like professionals tomorrow," she says in a no-nonsense tone. "No fooling around on the walkie-talkies. Got it?"

"Yeah," reply Timmy and Charlie. Adam gives a thumbs up.

Ella finds it hard to sleep later that night as she turns over all the gala details in her head. "Ahh!" she moans when she notes the 2:00 a.m. time on her nightstand's digital clock. After a few more tosses and turns, remembering her mother's advice for insomnia, she gets up and heads to the kitchen. Her mother always said that eating a complex carb like whole wheat bread helps trigger the release of the sleep-hormone serotonin.

After consuming the bread and a half glass of coconut milk, Ella heads back to bed and browses a magazine as she waits for the remedy to take effect. It only takes twenty minutes for her mother's medicine to do the trick, and Ella finally falls into a deep sleep. She wakes at five o'clock, just enough time to get washed and dressed before heading over to Firefly Lane Farm to meet Chef Frank and his crew.

"Ella!" Chef Frank, a pleasant man in his mid-forties, greets Ella with a bear hug at the entrance to the barn.

"Hey, Frank." Ella smiles. "Let's get you inside. I don't know about you, but I haven't had my coffee yet, and boy, do I need it today."

"I've already had my quota." Frank chuckles. "The rest of my crew will be coming shortly. Don't let me stop you from whatever you need to do. I've got my end covered, and just so you know, I'll be here until the event is over."

"Thank you. I'll be in my office taking care of some last-minute items. Just holler if you need anything."

After two cups of coffee and a breakfast of Greek yogurt and banana, items regularly stored in the office kitchen, Ella answers her cell phone.

"Morning, Ella. Carter here. How goes it?"

"Just taking care of some last-minute details."

"The event cocktail hour starts at six tonight, correct?"

"Yup."

"Would it be okay if I get there at seven-thirty or so? You mentioned I wouldn't be playing until after dinner—around eight-thirty, right?"

"You don't want to eat dinner?"

"I don't like to eat before I play. Afterward, though, it would be great, maybe when the DJ starts with the dance music. That is, if the chef will hold me a plate."

"I've arranged for you and your backup band to have a table, so I'll let Chef Frank know you will all be eating after you play."

"Perfect. Will you have time after the event to maybe hang out for a while?"

"I'm not sure, Carter. Can we play it by ear? I may crash after. It's been a whirlwind week."

"Okay. If I don't see you this evening, I want a raincheck."

"You got it. See you tonight." Ella presses the disconnect icon on her cell phone. Thinking about what to do about the two men in her life must go on the back burner until after the gala.

At four o'clock, Ella heads home to wash and dress for the evening's Christmas soirée. Conducting a final makeup and outfit check in her bedroom's full-length mirror, she is pleased at what she sees.

Not bad.

She looks breathtakingly stunning in her elegant, floor-length, form-fitting, off-the-shoulder, long-sleeved, red velvet gown paired with comfortable, red velvet pumps with a satin bow gracing the toe of each shoe. She accessorizes with her dangling diamond earrings and matching necklace—a birthday gift from her late husband, Jack.

"Okay, outta here," she tells the mirror and heads for the great room, where she removes a black velvet cape with a faux fur collar from a hanger in the hall closet. After putting on the cape, Ella grabs her black satin purse and keys from the hall table and heads for the garage.

Once in the car, she feels a jolt of energy when Harrison's name lights up on the car's console.

"Just calling to wish you a fantastic event," he tells her when she connects.

"I appreciate that."

"Luke and I, as well as the folks from the office, will be arriving around six. Text me should you need anything. Okay?"

"Okay, thank you, Harrison. See you soon."

That was so nice of Harrison to call, Ella thinks. His words bring her comfort, knowing he's got her back.

"Ella," Sophia calls when Ella arrives at Firefly Lane Farm. She looks beautiful in a cowl-neck, green satin gown accented with a sparkling emerald necklace and earrings. "You look so glam, *daahling!*"

Ella chuckles at her friend's greeting. "So do you."

"Ed," Sophia shouts to a young photographer loaded with camera gear at the other end of the room. "Can you take a two-shot of me and Ella by the Christmas tree?" Sophia points to the beautifully adorned tree at the entrance of the hall.

"Coming," Ed replies as he heads over to the ladies and snaps a roll of film.

"Do you need a printout of the shot sheet, Ed?" Ella asks as Sophia heads to another area of the hall to talk to the support staff.

"Nope. I printed it off your email. I'll make sure to get all the setups you requested—the sponsors, scholarship winners, each table, etcetera." He pulls a copy out of his shirt pocket and waves it.

"Great. Timmy at the guest reception desk has a walkie-talkie for you. Sophia, Adam Black, one of our staff volunteers, and I will also be on walkie-talkies, and Adam can help you with the photo setups. Just let one of us know if you need help with anything."

Ed gives a thumbs up.

"Ella, the carolers are here." Sophia waves to Ella in a "come here" gesture.

In the barn lobby, the carolers, dressed in beautiful Victorian clothing, stand by the nativity set that will greet guests as they enter the hall. They warm up performing "Hark! The Herald Angels Sing." Ed, the photographer, takes advantage of this beautiful photo op, and Ella and Sophia look on, pleased with their decision to hire the talented group.

Ella and Sophia clap after the carolers' song ends. "Timmy is on a walkie-talkie," Ella tells the head caroler as she points to Timmy, who sits at the guest check-in table with other volunteers. "Let him know if you need anything, and he'll contact me." The head caroler nods in understanding.

Twenty minutes later, guests begin to arrive for the cocktail hour, and the carolers start to sing their traditional list of well-loved Christmas hymns and carols.

With a walkie-talkie in hand, Ella greets guests as they arrive. Waiters and waitresses dressed in Victorian costumes take drink orders and pass trays of delectable appetizers.

"Rosemary, you look beautiful." Ella kisses Rosemary's cheek when her friend arrives.

Dressed in a pretty, long, white satin dress with gold trim and a pale blue satin shawl around her shoulders, Rosemary beams.

"You're positively radiant." Ella can't help but feel the loving energy her friend exudes. "Do you realize you're glowing?"

Rosemary smiles warmly and winks.

"I have you sitting at table seven with Adam, Timmy, Charlie, and their parents." Ella points to the reception desk and adds, "Timmy has your place card noting your dinner selection."

Rosemary turns to face Timmy, and he waves. "Wonderful, thank you, Ella." Rosemary heads toward the reception table as other guests say hello, convening around Ella.

"You look stunning," someone whispers in Ella's ear from behind. When she turns, she sees Harrison, and her heart skips a beat. "Harrison. A tux! You look great."

Dressed in a dark blue tuxedo jacket detailed with a floral jacquard pattern and a black satin lapel that makes his blue eyes pop, Harrison is indeed devastatingly handsome. The coat is fashionably paired with black pants, a white shirt, and a dark navy blue bow tie.

When Harrison tenderly kisses Ella's cheek, it almost makes her knees buckle. There is some serious kinetic chemistry taking place.

"Hey, hi, Ella," Luke Grant, also handsome in a black tux and bow tie, greets Ella and playfully smacks his brother's back. "And hello to you, too, bro."

The hall entrance now overflows with guests and others who greet Ella, including Lester and Penelope Sinclair and Doris and her husband, Larry.

"Lester and Penelope, I have you sitting with Doris and Larry. Timmy at reception will give you your place cards," Ella says as she points to Timmy at reception.

"I know you have a lot on your plate, " Harrison says to Ella. "I'll leave you to do whatever you must, but remember, save a dance for me."

When Harrison touches Ella's arm, another bolt of electricity runs through her. "I will," she replies as she feels herself blush.

Okay, Ella, get a grip.

An hour later, as the cocktail hour comes to a close, guests are ushered into the main hall to their tables for dinner. Father Paul delivers the dinner blessing at the microphone on stage, and afterward, the DJ plays soft ambient Christmas music to accompany dinner.

Halfway through dessert, Ella receives a text from Carter:

Parking the car now. – Carter

"You look fantastic!" Carter says as he meets Ella in the barn's front hall. He kisses her cheek.

"Thank you." Ella's genuinely happy to see Carter. He's handsome in his black pants, boots, and Western rodeo shirt with silver tooled floral embroidery around the shoulders and cuffs. Shortly after Carter greets Ella, five members of his backup band flow into the hall.

"Everyone here?" asks Ella.

Carter nods. "Yep."

"Let me take you backstage where you can set up." Ella takes the group around to a side entrance to the backstage area, which is kept private from the party guests. The band members, whose instruments were set out earlier, take their places behind the stage curtain to prepare for their performance.

Once the dessert plates are cleared, DJ Cory Michaels, an attractive, upbeat young man in a flashy tux, introduces Carter Huxley and his Blue River Broncos bandmates. The crowd goes wild, and for the next hour, folks sing along to Carter's well-known, Grammy-winning tunes and favorite holiday jingles.

"Thank you for being such a great audience, and a merry, blessed Christmas and happy holiday season to you all," Carter roars as the audience applauds with a standing ovation.

"That was amazing, Carter. Thank you so much." Ella and Carter embrace backstage.

"It was a good crowd. Glad I could do it."

"I have you and your band at table ten. So whenever you're ready, the waiters will serve dinner when you're seated."

"Thank you, Ella. I'll tell the guys, but if you don't mind, I'm going to head out. I don't want to my presence to take any attention away from the scholarship winners or anything you have planned."

"Are you sure?"

Carter nods. "I'll give you a ring tomorrow, though. I want to plan a time to get together. Okay?"

"Okay, sure."

"Thanks. Bye for now, then."

After Carter briefly kisses Ella, she takes a deep breath as she watches him go to his band members.

Just then Sophia comes into the backstage area. "Hey, Ella, ready to do the scholarship announcements?"

"Sure."

The two enter the stage from behind the curtain, take their places at the podium on stage right, introduce themselves, and thank the audience for their attendance and support.

"We'd also like to take this opportunity to present several scholarships—one winner each from Lavender Hill Cove's Elementary School, K through two classes—one for first grade, and one for grades three through five, as well as one winner each from Lavender Hill Cove's middle school and high school. Doris Banks, head librarian at our public library, will do the honors," Ella announces. "But first, Sophia and I would like to share why we felt the need to institute such a contest. Sophia, do you want to start?"

"Ella and I were saddened to see the vandalism of many of Lavender Hill Cove's retail store holiday displays, and there was also destruction of holiday decorations at private residences," Sophia begins. "We felt the need to bring to the community an awareness of the deeper meaning of Christmas and why we celebrate, as well as underscoring how the Good Lord, through the Golden Rule, wants us to treat our neighbors. You all know the rule: 'Do to others whatever you would have them do to you.'"

"There is a wonderful woman in attendance, an angel really, who gave us the idea to have Lavender Hill Cove's elementary, middle school, and high school students pick a Christmas-themed short story or book and share their thoughts about the meaning of the celebration— and with our K through two students, express this sentiment in a drawing," adds Ella. "That angel is Rosemary Engle. Rosemary, please stand."

Rosemary, blushing, stands and waves, surprised to be recognized. A wave of applause emanates from the crowd.

"Doris, please join Sophia, me, and the scholarship donors to present a fifteen-hundred-dollar scholarship to each of the winners," instructs Ella.

The group announces the four scholarships, with each student winner coming onto the stage to receive their awards. After that, photos of each winner and their scholarship sponsor are organized.

The first winner is a sweet K-2 girl, along with her representative from Michael's Grocery. Next, Ella presents a scholarship on behalf of Carter Huxley to an adorable fourth-grade boy. Third, Harrison presents a scholarship on behalf of Grant & Sons to a proud seventh grader, and a representative from the Knights of Columbus presents the final award to a happy tenth-grade girl. Green's Electronics then hands each scholarship winner a brand-new iPad wrapped in pretty holiday paper with substantial red bows. The crowd is told they can review all the winning essays at the library's website.

"And now, our DJ, Cory Michaels, takes the stage for the dance portion of the evening. Please, everyone, come and join us." Ella hands the microphone to Cory after announcing that the funds from the auction items and checks earmarked for those impacted by the recent vandalism will be split evenly among the town's victims.

"Ella," Harrison says, approaching her and taking her hand. "Let's dance."

Ella happily complies as she and Harrison join the assembled crowd on the dance floor.

"It was a great night, Ella," Harrison praises as guests leave the hall for home.

"Thank you for everything—your scholarship donation, your

support purchasing a table for your staff—"

"Of course. It was a wonderful community event. I believe it brought everyone together and you achieved your mission to underscore what Christmas is all about."

Ella smiles warmly at Harrison, who, holding her hand, takes it up to his mouth and kisses it.

"You sure I can't help you with anything?"

"No. Sophia, the event staff, and I have it covered," says Ella, shaking her head.

"Okay, then, I'll call you." Harrison lets go of Ella's hand and heads out with Luke and Grant & Son employees who have been mingling at the hall's exit.

After all guests leave, the event staff breaks down the tables and chairs and places them in the barn storage. The linens are put in laundry bags to be sent out on Monday morning. Chef Frank and his staff have already cleaned and put away all the glassware, china, and silverware.

"I think we can call it a wrap for tonight. We can take care of other details on Monday," Sophia says as she and Ella lock up.

"Hey, Sis," Ella calls, seeing Julie. "I thought you and Tom left."

"We did. I left my reading glasses on the table."

"Oh, those were yours? The glasses are in my office."

"Ladies, I'm going to bid you both adieu," Sophia says. "My feet hurt, and I'm about to keel over from exhaustion. So, night-night."

The ladies kiss and hug one another goodnight, and Ella and Julie retrieve Julie's glasses from Ella's office. Coming back toward the entrance, the two find Charlie and Timmy waiting in the hall, holding their walkie-talkies.

"You boys still here?" Ella asks, walking over to them, followed by Julie.

Moments later, Adam is heard yelling through the walkie-talkies. "There's a group of guys throwing snowballs and wrecking the Christmas decorations in front. Help me!"

Ella, Julie, and the boys jump to attention and run outside. They find Adam by the barn's holiday display, engaged in a scuffle with a group of masked youths.

Julie, sensing the urgency of the situation, immediately springs into action. She tackles the culprit, landing on Adam from behind. The other vandals, realizing they've been caught, hastily run off and pile into a sedan, its tires screeching as it speeds out of the near-empty parking lot.

Ella tries to help her sister and, in the scuffle, gets punched in the eye. "OW!"

When Julie pins down the disheveled teen, Adam squirms out from under the huddle.

In minutes, police cars arrive on the scene. Julie cuffs the wayward teen and reads him his rights as Adam, Charlie, and Timmy tend to Ella.

"I think you're going to have a real big shiner," Adam states.

"I hope it doesn't hurt too bad," commiserates Timmy.

"It's killing me." Ella, holding her injured eye, moans.

"Sis, you really got hit," Julie tells her. "I think I better take you to the ER."

"Okay," Ella acquiesces. "But let's just make sure the barn is locked up. Boys, is someone taking you home?"

As Ella asks the question, Charlie's dad pulls up in his van and asks what he can do to help.

"Just see that the boys get home safely," Julie says. "I'm taking my sister to the ER now."

"We'll call you tomorrow, Miss Ella, to see how you are," Adam promises as he, Timmy, and Charlie pile into the van.

Later that evening, after the ER visit, Ella is presented with her to-do list: 1) keep her head elevated to help decrease the swelling; 2) apply cold compresses for the first twenty-four hours; 3) apply an icepack for fifteen to twenty minutes at a time once an hour, then switch to warm compresses after the first twenty-four hours, and; 4) continue with the compresses until the swelling goes down. Other than turning shades of black, blue, and yellow, Ella is told she will be fine.

"Are you sure you don't want me to stay the night?" asks Julie once Ella is safely inside her home.

"I'll be okay. But I do need to get my car in the morning."

"No, give me your keys. Tom and I will pick up your car and bring it to you. You should not be driving."

Ella sighs. "Thanks, Sis. For everything. I'm glad you left your glasses. I don't know what I would have done if you hadn't been there."

Julie gives Ella a hug. "It was meant to be. Try to get some rest."

Heart Strings

"To love at all is to be vulnerable."

~C.S. Lewis

Chapter Thirteen

The following morning, after checking out the progress of her swollen left eye—not a pretty sight—Ella's phone rings. It's Julie.

"How are you feeling, Sis?"

"Like I got socked in the eye."

"Well, I want to let you know, the kid we arrested last night—he wound up giving up his buddies. Turns out they're the culprits who've been vandalizing the town."

"What's going to happen to them?"

"The court system will decide."

"Maybe they should all be made to write essays explaining the deeper meaning of Christmas."

"Maybe so. But they'll probably be behind bars when they do."

"Ouch."

"Well, all actions have consequences. But I called to tell you that Tom and I will be by later this morning with your car. In the meantime, I hope you don't mind, but I asked Rosemary to check on you."

Just then Ella's doorbell rings. "I think she's here now, Jules. I have to get the door. See you later."

"Oh, my dear." Rosemary sighs when she sees Ella's disfigured face. "Does it hurt much?"

"Some, but arnica, anti-inflammatory eye drops, and painkillers help."

"Tsk, tsk," empathizes Rosemary.

Ella sighs. "The good news is that I should be back to normal in maybe a week or so."

"Well, I brought you your favorite—a batch of my pumpkin-chocolate chip muffins, baked fresh this morning." Rosemary holds up the basket of muffins.

"Yum. Thank you. Care to join me in a cup of coffee and a muffin? I haven't had breakfast yet."

"Don't mind if I do."

"Sometimes, I marvel at the timing of things," Ella comments as she brews the coffee.

Rosemary sets Ella's kitchen table with breakfast plates and silverware. "How so?"

"My sister left her reading glasses on our table at the gala. While we were breaking down the room, I noticed them and, not realizing they were hers, put them in my office in case someone came looking for them. However, Julie returned just as I was about to leave for home, and it's a good thing she did. She was there when the vandals attacked and was able to apprehend one of the culprits. I think she also saved me and the boys from more harm."

"Frightening."

"You can say that again."

"I think your angels were in high gear that night."

"Huh?" asks Ella, deep in thought, sipping her hot drink.

"You believe in angels?"

"Of course, yes."

"Well, they protected you from something worse than a black eye."

Ella thinks about this. "I believe that."

"Psalm Ninety-one says, "For he will order his angels to protect you wherever you go," Rosemary cites. "Everyone has a guardian angel or two." She winks. "Angels can be wonderfully helpful in so many ways. Unfortunately, not too many people call on them for help. If only they did—the angels are waiting and only too happy to oblige."

An hour after Rosemary has returned home, Ella gets a text. It's from Carter.

> I heard on the news about the attack after the gala. Are
> you okay?

Ella texts back:

Just a big swollen eye that's turning menacing colors.

Carter responds:

So sorry to hear that. What a terrible scare that scene must have been. Feel better soon. I'm headed into Manhattan today for a meeting. I'll call you when I land. Thinking of you. XO – Carter

Moments later, Ella receives another text. It's Harrison.

Ella, I'm in front of your house. I heard about you getting hurt. I brought you something. If you want, I can come back later.

Ella texts back:

It's okay, come up to the door.

Ella gets up from the sofa and looks at herself in the hall mirror. She's wearing jeans and a comfortable, oversized, soft pink sweater. While her hair still looks fabulous, her face is a mess. Nothing can help that, so when Harrison knocks, she opens the door.

Harrison gasps when he sees Ella's face. "Oh, no," he says with sympathy. He hands her some flowers and a bag with the Love Street Bakery logo. "As soon as I heard, I just had to see you. I hope you don't mind that I just dropped by."

"No worries. Come on in. The flowers are gorgeous, thank you." Peeking into the bag, she adds, "And muffins. Yum!"

"I know how much you like the pumpkin-chocolate chip muffins from Love Street."

Ella laughs out loud.

"What's so funny?"

"My neighbor Rosemary made me some pumpkin-chocolate chip muffins and brought them over earlier."

"Well, now you'll be fully stocked for a while."

Ella chuckles. "Can I offer you coffee . . . *and a muffin?*" They both laugh.

"Sure."

Harrison follows Ella into the kitchen as she unwraps the bouquet, revealing a stunning array of red and white roses, along with artificial berries on stems, glittering pine cones, and greenery. She places the arrangement in a tall red vase, after which she and Harrison sit in the kitchen nook while the coffee brews.

"I was worried about you." Harrison gently places his hand over Ella's.

"Thank you. And thank you for the muffins." Ella chuckles nervously again. "I must look awful."

"You're beautiful even with a black eye."

"Oh, I don't know about that." Ella makes a face. "I think the coffee's ready. Would you like to join me in the great room? I was preparing to watch *It's a Wonderful Life*."

"Ah, the classic Frank Capra movie with Jimmy Stewart and Donna Reed. I'd love to watch it with you."

Ella and Harrison take their coffee mugs and muffins and sit side by side on Ella's big, comfortable sofa. With the TV remote in hand, Ella navigates to the movie and hits the play button.

Twenty minutes into the film, Harrison naturally takes Ella's hand. Ella smiles, and when Harrison pulls her close, she rests her head on his chest.

Watching the film with Harrison in the soothing warmth of her great room, by the sparkling lights of the Christmas tree and a gas fire roaring in the hearth, Ella, feeling much better, smiles, utterly contented.

Days later, as Ella prepares for her evening date with Carter, she frowns at her reflection in the bathroom mirror. Despite her favorite foundation, a hint of bruising under her eye can still be seen. She retrieves a jar of professional cover-up cream from her vanity drawer and delicately applies the silky miracle cosmetic. As if by magic, the discoloration disappears, leaving her face flawless. Pleased with the transformation, Ella selects a reddish-pink lipstick to complement her hot-pink, buttoned-down satin shirt and straight-legged black dress pants that she has paired with black bootlets. Moments later, an incoming text pings on her cell phone.

I'm on my way. See you in five. – Carter

Ella texts back a thumbs up emoji dabs a bit of jasmine essential oil behind each ear, and heads toward her front hall closet to retrieve her coat. Moments later, the doorbell rings.

Carter, as usual, is drop-dead handsome in a black turtleneck, black leather coat, and jeans. "Love your pink satin top."

"Why, thank you." Ella, her movements graceful and deliberate, slips into a chic charcoal-gray cashmere jacket and wraps a delicate powder-pink scarf around her neck. She and Carter then step out of her home, ready for the evening.

"Nice car," admires Ella as she slides into the passenger seat of Carter's sleek Gentian blue metallic Porsche. "Is it new?"

"My Christmas present to myself."

"Hmm. You treat yourself quite nice, Santa," Ella teases, a playful glint in her eye.

Carter laughs.

"How many cars do you own?"

"Only three—my Jeep, my truck, and this baby."

"Nice."

Carter winks.

"I'm looking forward to the Eagle's Nest tonight. Besides the gala, it's been a while since I've danced."

"Me too." He reaches for the car's radio and turns on soft instrumental music. "Congratulations on the success of the gala. I hear they'll break ground on the library's new wing sometime in the spring."

"That's the plan. I want to thank you as well. Your contribution made ticket sales soar. Sophia and I really appreciate your support."

"You're welcome. Hey, your eye looks all healed."

Ella chuckles. "The magic of makeup. I'm still a little black and blue, but the dermatologic cover-up works great."

"Well, I'm glad they caught the culprits and that you're on the mend."

"How about you? How's everything going with the album?"

"We're preparing to shoot a music video, and we have an extensive marketing campaign in the works. So all's good. We're on track."

"Good to hear. Will you be traveling?"

"Not until just before the album's released, so I'm sure you'll get sick of me."

"I doubt that." Ella smiles.

Carter returns the smile and places his right hand over Ella's, which is resting on her knee. His touch causes Ella to inhale deeply—they have history, and there's that chemistry again.

Carter pulls up to the valet at the Eagle's Nest and hands the parking attendant a tip to keep a keen eye on his car.

"Sure thing, Mr. Huxley," the admiring teen, an obvious fan, gushes.

The sophisticated venue creates a romantic setting with wood paneled walls made of the finest cherry, soft ambient lighting, and cozy table seating. A hostess walks Carter and Ella to their table, where they have a prime view of the stage and dance floor. The pretty hostess lights the candles on their table and informs them that their waiter will be by momentarily.

After ordering a vintage bottle of French Chardonnay, Carter also orders the club's signature jumbo shrimp and lobster appetizer. "To the season and you." Carter and Ella clink their wine glasses.

"This is lovely, Carter. Thank you." Ella lathers a baguette slice with brie cheese and caramelized pecan topping. "I better watch it, or I won't be able to eat dinner."

"Eat what you like, and I hope you still like to dance because we'll be doing much of that tonight."

Ella grins. "I'm game."

I could get used to this.

While it's a bit nerve-wracking dating two men, she is comforted by following the advice of not only Sophia but her mother and sister, who all insist that she enjoy the dating process as a means to get to know the man, and then, whomever steps up and indicates they want exclusivity and have the same values and plan for the future, only then should she choose.

"Come on, I love this old Nat King Cole tune. Let's get a dance in before our salads arrive." The band leader is singing the opening lines to "Unforgettable." Carter takes Ella's hand as they head for the dance floor.

Carter holds Ella close as they slowly move to the beat. Looking up into his eyes, she feels her knees start to buckle. When Carter places a tender kiss on her neck, she almost gasps.

"Carter—" Ella begins.

But before she has a chance to say more, he places a gentle kiss on her lips. The kiss lasts seconds but makes a powerful impact.

Once back at their table, the salads are delivered. Ella is determined to slow things down with Carter. While enjoying the evening, she is resolute about not rushing into a committed relationship. After eating a few bites of her salad, she decides to assert her boundaries if Carter tries to kiss her again. She wants to take things slow and ensure she doesn't give him the wrong impression that she's "his girl."

"What are your plans for Christmas?" Carter asks and takes a sip of his wine.

"We're gathering at my parents' place on Christmas Eve. It's a family tradition. And you?"

"My family celebrates Christmas Eve, too. It would be nice to spend part of the holiday together, either Christmas Eve or day."

Ella takes another bite of her salad and a sip of wine, wondering how to answer. "Christmas Day is possible. Are you planning to go to church?"

"Church? Uh—" Carter hesitates. "I'm not sure. I haven't been in a while."

"No?"

Carter shakes his head. "Are you going?"

"I plan to. I go every Sunday."

Carter is quiet.

"Oh, I'm not asking you to go with me; I just wanted to know if you were going."

"Let me get back to you on that. Wow, dinner looks incredible!" Carter quickly changes the subject as the waiter puts before them their plates of pesto salmon with potatoes au gratin and string beans almondine.

"It sure does," Ella agrees. She works to hide her disappointment that Carter doesn't seem to share her views on church attendance.

Over dinner, the conversation turns to lighter fare, focusing mainly on Carter's music, Ella's business, and local news.

"Would you like to do this again, maybe mid-week on Wednesday?" Carter asks. "They're having a Christmas concert at the North Fork Vineyards. It's going to be a blast! We could grab a bite beforehand." Carter has his arm around Ella's waist as he walks her to her front door and his eyes light up with excitement as he makes the suggestion.

"I'd like that," Ella replies. "I'd invite you in, but—"

"No night cap?" ask Carter with a boyish pout.

"I've got to get up early tomorrow." Ella puts her key into the door lock.

"It's the weekend."

"I know, but I promised Sophia that I'd help her take care of a few things in the morning."

"Ella—" Carter leans in for a kiss, persistent.

"Carter." Ella stops him with a gentle hand to his chest. "I need to take things slow. We're still finding things out about one another."

"But—"

"I know we have history, but we're different people now. Let's start fresh and get to know who we are today, as if we just met. Are you okay with that?"

Carter runs his hands through his hair. He is obviously somewhat

disappointed; however, he manages to crack a small smile. "Okay."
After a beat he asks, "See you Wednesday?"

Ella nods as she opens her door. "Good night."

"Don't I even get a hug?"

Ella hugs Carter and they share a brief kiss. "Till Wednesday,"
she says as she turns the key and enters the house.

The following day, Ella and Sophia finish labeling boxes and
organizing Firefly Lane Farm's storage room shelves, which hold with
the remainder of the Christmas gala decorations and sundry items for
safekeeping until next year's event.

"Excellent. We are finito!" Sophia exclaims as she glances at the
time on the wall clock. "Three o'clock. Looks like it's teatime."

"I could use a cup."

Inside the barn's kitchen, Sophia fills the electric teapot with
water while Ella looks through the selection of tea packets in a large
wicker basket on the countertop.

"What'll it be? Lemon ginger, Earl Grey, tropical green tea—"

"Yes to the green tea."

"For me, too," replies Sophia.

Ella unwraps the packets and places a tea bag into each of the two
mugs stamped with the Firefly Lane Farm Catering and Events logo.

"So, you mentioned you had a nice time on your date with Carter,
but I sense something's up." Sophia blows on her hot tea as she and
Ella sit at one of the kitchen tables.

"We had a lot of fun. We have good chemistry, but . . ."

"But what?"

"But—" Ella chuckles nervously, remembering. "After dinner,
when Carter dropped me off at home, he wanted to come inside for a
nightcap."

"Yeah, I bet. And?"

"I said I needed to get up early, that I had to help you today."

"Oh, yeah, blame it on me." Sophia laughs, her eyes twinkling with mischief.

"Sophia—"

"Just kidding."

"I told him that even though we have history, we've both changed so much, and we have to start fresh as if we just met. And I reminded him again that I want to take it slow. And although I didn't tell him this, I want to make sure he's sincere about what he told me about being ready to share his life with someone."

"Well, you're very wise to take it slow. It's not easy to do when there's chemistry."

"That's precisely when it's needed most. I've always been extremely attracted to Carter. I want to kiss him, and yes, when I do, it feels good. But Harrison feels good, too. It's not a simple choice; it feels like a tug-of-war going on in my heart and head."

Sophia bursts out laughing. "Such problems."

"Oh, cut it out."

"Sorry, my bad." Sophia laughs out loud.

Ella taps Sophia's arm her playfully. "The truth is I like them both. I know Carter better, but Harrison is still a mystery."

"And Carter hurt you when he said he was ready and it turned out he wasn't. Do you think he's changed? Is he being honest with himself, or does he want to be with you in any way he can? You're the one who must be discerning. Most men would like to be your boyfriend."

"You're just prejudiced."

"Seriously, Ella, you're a prize. You need to hold firm to your wishes and values and see who best fits you."

"I know. I know." Ella sips her tea. "I need more time. I also think I'm still grieving over Jack."

"That may be true, so taking it slow is definitely the best way forward. However, Jack also hurt you, even though you two were on your way to patching things up before he died. Do you think that's influencing you in any way?"

Ella ponders Sophia's question and takes another sip of her tea. "I . . . I don't know. Maybe."

"Do you think you might be afraid to let go and let yourself love again?"

"Hmm." Ella shrugs. "I'll have to deeply ponder that concept."

As the two friends spend time enjoying their tea and talking about their hopes and plans for the future, even though no resolution is in sight, Ella feels better for having shared with her friend.

"My parents couldn't stop raving about the great time they had at the Once Upon a Cove Christmas Gala. That's why we wanted to come by and see the venue. I'm so glad we did. This is the perfect place for a summer wedding," gushes Sienna Joseph, a young bride-to-be, as she co-signs the catering agreement with her fiancé, Nicholas Chase. The couple's excitement is palpable, and it always makes Ella feel great and gives her tremendous satisfaction when she can help couples and families plan important life events.

After the couple leaves her office, Ella receives a text from Harrison:

> Morning, Ella. I've been thinking about you 😊 and wondering if you'd be available for an impromptu lunch today. The Cove's Ice Palace has a beautiful holiday display and a lunch and skating package where they provide you with ice skates—that is if you're game. If not, we can do lunch at the Seaside Bistro.

Ella looks at the clock on her office wall, which reads ten o'clock and texts Harrison back:

> Ice-skating. What fun! Would love to go to the Ice Palace. Want to say one o'clock?

Harrison replies:

> Fantastic. I'll drop by around twelve fifty.

Ella sits at her computer for the next few hours, answering emails and coordinating future conference dates with prospective customers. At around half past twelve, Sophia knocks on Ella's door jamb. "Hey, girlfriend, what're you doing for lunch today? Want to walk over to my house and fix something?"

"I can't, sorry, Soph. Harrison's picking me up just before one o'clock."

"Oh, that's nice."

"He called and asked me, spur of the moment, if I was available and said he's been thinking of me."

Sophia flashes Ella an approving thumbs up. "You know, since I've been vicariously living through your dating life, I started thinking about Harrison's brother, Luke, and I'm wondering that it might be nice if we all get together again—something casual that doesn't feel like a date or that we're being fixed up."

"Ahh, I see." Ella trills enthusiastically, excited at the prospect. "I think that can definitely be arranged."

"You were right on the dot." Ella compliments Harrison on his promptness. He has picked her up exactly when he said he would, at ten minutes to the hour.

"Yup, it's a habit of mine. At work, I make it a point to arrive at our construction sites on time and set a good example for my crew."

"Very admirable." Ella winks, her eyes sparkling with mischief.

The playful banter, a dance of words and wit, continues until Harrison pulls his truck into the Ice Palace's parking lot.

"I haven't been on the ice in years!" Ella chuckles, excited about the prospect. "I'm glad I dressed for the occasion." She is wearing slim-fitted leggings and a long sweater underneath her knee-length wool parka. "I just hope I can remember how to skate."

"It's like riding a bike."

"I hope so. What made you think of ice-skating?"

"My company recently remodeled the venue. I thought it might be fun to check out all the holiday decorations, which I understand are quite extensive—a winter wonderland, if you will. And then, as we skate, we can hold hands." Harrison winks playfully and laughs.

"Oh, I see, ulterior motives. Hmm. I've got your number."

They both laugh out loud.

"This is amazing!" Ella gushes after Harrison pays their entry fees and they head to the rink in their skates.

Surrounding the oval-shaped rink is an alpine gingerbread village, a nostalgic throwback to Christmases of old. The town sits on carpets of sparkling white cotton mica to resemble a snow-covered landscape. Pine trees dusted with white flock spray sparkle with lights, and there are charming cottages, a general store, a church with a steeple, candy canes with red bows, old-fashioned streetlights aglow, and a host of waving villagers in Bavarian-style clothing. The entire scene is filled with the festive spirit as holiday music plays. Santa, holding the reins of his red sleigh perched in the sky is led by his reindeer, with Rudolph's glowing nose leading the pack. It's an amazing site to behold.

"A winter wonderland, indeed. The display is more elaborate than I imagined." Harrison reaches out his hand for Ella to hold as they enter the rink.

"Ooh, I'm a little unsteady."

"I've got you," Harrison promises, and still holding Ella's hand, he puts an arm around her waist.

"Okay, I think my memory of being on the ice has returned," Ella says as they start their second pass around the rink.

"You're doing great."

"How did you become such a skilled skater?"

"Ice hockey was a favorite sport of mine growing up."

"Ah, I see. Sailing, watersports, snow skiing—you're quite the outdoorsman."

Harrison winks at her again.

"I'm glad you said yes to getting together today. You made my day." Harrison imitates Clint Eastwood's signature line with perfection.

Ella laughs again. "This is really fun," she says after they skate several more laps. "Harrison, I was wondering—"

Harrison looks at Ella, eyebrows slightly raised, waiting for her to continue.

"Remember when you, Luke, Sophia, and I went to that concert in the park?"

Harrison nods.

"Sophia mentioned she had such a good time, and so did I. It would be great if we could all do something like that again."

"Well, the concerts in the park are only held in the spring and summer—"

A rush of thoughts on how best to pursue Sophia's request rush through Ella's mind.

Before she can say more, Harrison continues. "Luke and I talked about going into Manhattan for dinner and take in the holiday sights, and perhaps the Christmas show at Radio City. How does that sound? Do you think you'd both like to join us?"

"That would be great. I know Sophia would love it." Ella knows something like this is just what Sophia had in mind. "I haven't been to Radio City in decades, and the city at Christmas is magical."

"Great. I'll look into getting tickets and get back to you."

After skating, Ella and Harrison grab a bite at the Ice Palace's picturesque restaurant, a charming cottage-style bistro situated on a private inlet with a breathtaking view of Peconic Bay. It has a cozy, casual atmosphere and delectable fare ranging from soups and salads to paninis and other delicious selections.

"What'll it be?" a waitress asks. She's a little heavyset, older than most waitresses, and wears her dyed chestnut hair in a bun, but she has a jovial face. Her nametag that reads "Dolly."

Harrison and Ella both order ice teas, which Dolly promptly brings. After perusing the menu, they both order a bowl of New England Clam chowder, and two Caesar salads topped with grilled chicken. Their order comes with a basket of freshly baked cornbread

"I love the view." Ella remarks after Dolly heads for the kitchen to place their orders.

"So do I." Harrison agrees, looking directly at Ella.

Ella laughs and returns the gaze. "Yeah, my view isn't so bad either."

"Do you think you might have a few extra minutes to take a walk by the water and the pier out there after we finish eating?" Harrison looks out the restaurant window toward a long pier off the nearby sandy beach. "There's nothing like a good walk after a meal. and it's such a gorgeous day. Unusually warm for this time of year."

"You're on!"

Walking along the beach toward the pier, Harrison reaches for Ella's hand. Ella likes that Harrison is about a foot taller than she and enjoys the feel of his large hand around her tiny one. His body temperature runs several degrees warmer than hers, and she finds that comforting as well. In fact, she feels quite protected and at ease around him.

"Ella, I, um—" Harrison, usually composed, stutters, and Ella senses his vulnerability. "After the gala, when I heard that you were hurt—" Harrison's tone changes to serious. "When I heard that you were hurt, I got so worried. It made me think—a lot."

"I know you were concerned, and I appreciate that."

"I really like you, Ella." Harrison pauses for a beat. "Really like you. I'm falling . . . hard."

Ella is stunned. She doesn't know how to respond.

"We're not in high school, so I can't exactly ask you to go steady," Harrison continues. "But I would like to be exclusive. I'm not interested in dating anyone else. I've told you where I'm coming from: I want a life partner, marriage, and, hopefully, kids. On one of our first dates, you said that's what you want, too. What do you think? Shall we take it one day at a time and see where it goes?" Harrison's sincerity is unmistakable, making Ella feel secure.

As Ella looks into Harrison's blue eyes, she can feel herself welling up with emotion. While she cares for Carter, she feels lighter and happier with Harrison. Carter doesn't make her feel like Harrison does—cherished, secure, and protected. Harrison is not just mindful of

Ella's feelings, he truly understands her, and he's generous, considerate, reliable, and honest, which makes her feel the same way. She and Harrison share the same values, goals, and, most importantly, the same devotion to their faith. In choosing Harrison, Ella knows that God will play an essential role in their lives, making all the difference for a solid foundation on which to build a life together. She knows Harrison is available to her—unlike Carter, whose career and fame often take priority. However, she's not ready to commit, not yet.

"Harrison, I really like you too. I feel so good with you, and comfortable, and I appreciate that we share the same values and are on the same page about so many things. However, I've been through a tough time with the loss of my husband, and I'm still working through a few things. I didn't expect to have this conversation with you so soon. I would love to continue to see you, but would you mind if get back to you with my answer about exclusivity?"

"Of course. I don't want to rush you. I want you to be sure."

Ella squeezes his hand and then brings it to her lips and kisses it. Suddenly—she doesn't know why—but she feels like crying. Instead, she holds back her tears and wraps her arms around Harrison's waist and gives him a brief hug.

The two continue walking arm in arm toward the pier until Harrison spies a unique shell sticking out of the sand. "Look." He pulls the white shell out of the sand. He opens the shell and holds up the two halves, which meet in the middle, resembling two distinct wings.

"Angel Wings!" exclaims Ella.

"For you." Harrison places the find in Ella's hand and wraps his hand around hers as Ella envelops the angel wings.

Revelations

"It is love alone that gives worth to all things."

~St. Teresa of Avila

Chapter Fourteen

Ella, Rosemary, Charlie, Timmy, and Adam sit ensconced around the large wood table in Rosemary's kitchen as Christmas tunes play on Adam's tablet. They decorate a variety of gingerbread cookies, each shape adding to the festive spirit—from gingerbread men and women to Christmas trees, round ornaments, snowflakes, and angels.

Ella squeezes green icing out of a long piping bag fitted with a small round tip to add white accents to a Christmas tree.

"Decorating gingerbread cookies is fun," admits Adam having never had the experience. The other boys agree.

"Well, I'm glad you boys could join Ella and I. Making and decorating gingerbread cookies is an essential holiday activity."

"I agree whole-heartedly," states Ella.

"Hey, Timmy, can you hand me the red icing when you're done?" asks Adam as Timmy finishes placing red buttons on a gingerbread man.

"These cookies smell so good. Can we eat some when we're finished decorating?" asks Charlie.

"One each," states Rosemary as she trims an angel's wings with white icing in a pretty pattern. "The rest are for Christmas Day." Rosemary generously has invited Ella, the boys, and their families to Christmas Day brunch.

"What else will we be having?" asks Adam with anticipation.

"Oh, I'll be making my famous homemade Belgium waffles with whipped cream and strawberries, some egg dishes, among other treats." Rosemary winks.

"I'm bringing the bagels and cream cheese," adds Charlie.

"I know my Mom is baking something, I'm not sure what," offers Timmy.

"I'm going to help my Mom make apple pie—and we'll bring some ice cream, too," raves Adam.

"I hope we don't sugar overload." Ella laughs as she decorates a snowflake cookie.

After the boys are picked up by Timmy's father, Ella helps Rosemary clean up.

"That was fun. The boys had a blast, too. It's so kind of you to have us all over for Christmas brunch."

"The more, the merrier. I decided on brunch because I know people have other family commitments."

"Thank you."

"You mentioned to me that you've been dating, is there anyone you'd like to invite?"

"Well—" Ella stalls.

Rosemary looks Ella in the eye. "I hope you know you can tell me anything."

Ella nods. She knows Rosemary is a safe haven. Ella finally relays her dilemma—what to do about Carter and Harrison. She explains that she has a history with Carter, although he once led her to believe they had a future but then left her in the dust, but now he's returned and it appears he's sincere and they're on the same page. On the other hand, Harrison, whom she is just getting to know, is also someone she has much in common with and that she is strongly attracted to.

"I feel as if I'm going to have to decide soon. Both men have expressed interest in dating me and want commitment."

"Are you leaning toward one more than the other?"

"I'm confused. I'm also scared. Sophia said that maybe, because of the difficulties in my relationship with Jack, even though he eventually recognized the value of our relationship and what we shared, I might be afraid to be vulnerable to loving another."

"What do you think?"

"When I go deep inside, I think she may be right. I don't want to make the wrong choice. I want to know who a man is before I commit, not just who he says he is."

"You want to make sure he has the same values, the same commitment, and that your on the same path together."

"Yes."

Rosemary pauses to think the says, "It's an important decision. It's okay to take your time and to listen and observe. I believe you'll know the right choice to make at the right time. Pray. Ask the Lord for guidance to make the right choice and accept His will for your life."

"Thank you, Rosemary. You always know the right thing to say and do."

Rosemary chuckles. "Well, I do have somewhat of a special connection to the man upstairs." She winks, and Ella laughs with her.

"Yes, you do, Rosemary. Yes, you do."

Later that evening, at home, tucked comfortably in her bed, Ella thinks about her conversation with Rosemary and, following her friend's advice, begins praying aloud.

"Lord, I am confused. I'm unsure of the right decision or your will regarding Carter or Harrison. You know, better than I, my desires and what is best for me and my life. I hand myself over entirely to you. Please show me the way. Guide me to the best possible partner for my life, to the one where we can grow deeper in love all the days of our lives while keeping in your graces and in your light. Give me a sign, so that without a doubt, I will know the right choice."

"I've got some good news," Ella declares, grinning from ear to ear as she walks into Sophia's office the following morning and plops in a chair before her friend's desk.

Sophia looks up from her computer, all ears.

"Harrison managed to snag some exclusive tickets for us to Friday's Radio City show."

"Way to go. I love how you casually dropped the request into your lunch conversation. That was brilliant."

"And the best part? After the show, they're treating us to dinner at Il Colibri (the hummingbird), a new chic Italian restaurant in Uptown," Ella adds with a smile, knowing how much Sophia loves Italian food.

"I've read some great reviews about that place. I hear that inside; it looks like a garden with images of hummingbirds everywhere."

"It sounds lovely, and it's rated with three Michelin stars. It should be a great night."

"Speaking of men. Isn't tonight your North Fork Vineyard date with Carter?"

Ella nods.

"Gee, girl, I can barely keep up with your social calendar. I insist that you call me immediately after your date. I want to hear all about it."

"Maybe."

"Maybe?"

"Like I've told you before, I don't kiss and tell."

"Ha, ha. We'll see about that," says Sophia playfully as she turns back toward her computer to answer emails.

That evening, Ella drives toward the North Fork Vineyards just before dusk after Carter, delayed due to a business meeting close to the venue, lets Ella know to meet him there. In a way, Ella is relieved, as she can drive herself home and not have to face the possibility of Carter asking to come inside for a nightcap.

The North Fork Vineyards, a classic New England-style winery with a gabled roof, double-hung windows, and impressive double-door entry, is situated on forty acres of gorgeous country. Inside, a great hall leads to a wine-tasting room to the right, and to the left a restaurant with a bar and stage boasting picturesque views of the carefully tended to surrounding vineyards.

Rather than taking a seat at a restaurant table, the reservation being under Carter's name, Ella instead makes her way toward the lounge area and takes a seat on a plush leather seat at a tabletop near the beautiful mahogany bar.

A perky blonde waitress dressed in a short skirt, white silk buttoned-down top and sexy stilettos greets Ella and takes her Chardonnay drink order.

"Hello. My name is Tammy. Are you part of the Wyndham Group?" asks the waitress as she places Ella's drink on a napkin in front of her along with a small bowl of warm mixed nuts.

"No, I'm meeting my date, Carter Huxley."

"Oh, Carter, yes, ah, you'll be seated in the dining room where they're having the holiday concert."

"Yes."

"Well, we'll be sure to take care of your table. Don't hesitate to call on myself or Angela." Tammy points to Angela taking another patron's order. "I'll let our bartender Billy knows you're with Carter." Tammy picks up the black leather restaurant bill fold. "We'll put this on Carter's tab. Tell him Tammy says, hello."

Ella takes a sip of her Chardonnay and watches as Tammy walks away. Her swagger a bit more pronounced than it was earlier. Moments later, she receives a text from Carter that he's on his way.

"Hey, babe," Carter greets Ella with a kiss on the cheek when he arrives. "Want to take our seat inside the restaurant? It's a lot more comfortable."

"Sure." Ella nods and, taking her drink, follows Carter into the restaurant. He heads toward what Ella learns shortly is known to be "his table."

"Hi, Carter," coos Tammy, all smiles when she walks by Carter and Ella's table.

"How have you been?" asks Carter.

"Doing well. We've missed you around here."

"Well, I've been busy working on the next album."

"I can't wait to hear it." Tammy smiles a gorgeous white, toothy smile. Suddenly Ella feels left out and squirms a little in her chair.

"Here's the wine list, Carter. I'll be back in a few to take your order, unless you know what you want now," says Tammy a bit too seductively.

"Thanks. I'll look it over. Give me a few minutes."

"Will do." Tammy turns and there's that swagger again.

It's a wonder she doesn't trip and break her neck on those heels.

Ella chuckles under her breath. Tammy's come-on to Carter is so obvious. Carter takes it all in stride, obviously used to this type of attention.

The Surf and Turf dinner is superb, and Ella finds the conversation with Carter flowing quite nicely.

"Again, I'm sorry I couldn't pick you up at your home tonight."

"No worries, I understand when important business calls."

"I appreciate it." Carter places his hand over Ella's. "You look beautiful tonight," compliments Carter. Ella is stunning in an aqua-blue long-sleeved silk dress with a scoop neck. Her diamond teardrop earrings sparkle, illuminated by the table's candlelight.

The holiday music, performed by a well-loved local group, the Stardust Band, features a male and female vocalist, and is superb. The band plays all the romantic and popular holiday tunes of yesteryear as well as more modern tunes, but all with a distinct, smooth and jazzy style.

As they listen to the music, Carter pulls Ella close and, holding one of her hands, runs his other down Ella's back. At one point, he looks with such tenderness into her eyes, which makes Ella melt. She gives in to a delicious kiss; after all, they are in a private booth away from prying eyes.

Once the band takes a break, Ella and Carter share new bits about friends and people from their past.

"Oh, I heard through the grapevine Rory Thomas and Cynthia

Land are getting married," shares Ella. After moving away and losing their spouses, Rory and Cynthia, who went to high school with Ella and Carter, found each other again online.

"Oh, really?"

"Isn't that great? They both were so devastated by the loss of their spouses, it's great they reconnected after so many years, and that it's worked out the way it did."

"I guess so." Carter takes a forkful of his crème brulée.

"What do you mean?"

"Well, if it's good for them," says Carter somewhat sarcastic.

"You don't sound so happy for them." Ella chuckles nervously.

"Marriage is not right for everyone."

Ella's stomach turns.

Did he really say that just now?

"No, marriage isn't right for everyone, but it seems like it is for them."

"Well, good," says Carter, his expression unreadable, as he continues to eat his dessert. Ella, however, notices a hint of tension in his shoulders and a slight furrow in his brow.

"Where do you see yourself in the next few years, Carter?" asks Ella in a streak of boldness.

Carter looks up from his dessert.

"You mentioned on one of our dates recently that you've changed and you're thinking more about sharing your life with one person. Do you still feel that way?" Ella's voice is steady, her eyes unwavering as she asks the question.

"Ah, yeah." He doesn't sound convincing. "I believe in living together first; that way, you can see how things fit. Then maybe later—maybe, and I say that with a big M, *maybe marriage*. To tell you the truth, I don't see how a piece of paper plays such an important role."

Ella inhales deeply. She takes a sip of wine for fortification.

"I don't believe in living together before marriage. I think it goes against God's teaching. In fact, I know it does."

"You're kidding? Isn't that kind of an old-fashioned way of thinking? I mean, *this is the twenty-first century.*"

Ella clears her throat and firmly states. "It's what I believe."

Ella's mind is whirling. Her balance is off.

Is Carter gaslighting me? Didn't he tell me he wanted to share his life with one woman that night we ate at the Sandpiper? He went on about his best buddy Jackson's illness and said that it caused him to rethink his life.

Then suddenly, like being hit by lightning, Ella remembers.

Carter said he wanted to share his life, but maybe he meant living together, and not marriage. Well, wow. What a revelation.

"Would you excuse me for a minute, I need to go to the men's room. I'll be right back," says Carter, the conversation too intense for him.

Ella nods. When the waiter comes to the table to check on things, Ella orders a cappuccino. She needs a bolt of caffeine as a pick-me-up, a lifeline in this sea of confusion.

After her cappuccino arrives, Ella, having sorted through more of her thoughts, feels more grounded. However, she's keenly aware that Carter has been gone for some twenty or so minutes.

Ella heads toward the ladies' room and walks through the bar area. At the counter, she sees Carter and Tammy talk. They are all smiles, and both are seemingly in high flirt mode, although Tammy is the worst, practically gushing over every word out of Carter's mouth. It turns Ella's stomach. Then out of the blue, as she watches, Tammy places a kiss on Carter's mouth and slips him her number, which Carter places in the pocket of his pants. Ella feels as if she's been punched in the stomach. Holding in her true feelings, she walks toward Carter.

"Carter, I'm headed to powder my nose."

Carter suddenly, takes his distance from Tammy. "Okay, I'll meet you back at the table."

"Would you like anything else?" asks Carter when Ella returns to the table and sits.

"No, thank you." Then, after a few quiet moments, Ella continues. "Carter, you know how much I care for you. I've always felt a strong connection. I really want to thank you for the lovely dates we've been on of late, but I want to be honest with you. I was under the impression that when you talked about sharing your life with someone, you were talking about sharing your life—at some point—married."

"Maybe…possibly."

"But you've told me that you prefer living together first. There's no room for that in my life. It's not my value system. I don't think we're a good fit."

Carter stares at Ella, surprised, but he sees she's resolute.

"And, seeing you with Tammy, I think you still enjoy playing the field."

"She slipped me her number, but—"

"No need to explain. You don't have to. We're not committed to each other; we don't owe each other anything."

"Ella—".

"It's okay. However, I'm kind of tired, I think I'm going to head out." Ella kisses Carter on the cheek. "No hard feelings, really. Friends?"

Carter breathes in deeply, finally coming to terms with the status of their relationship. "Friends."

"Wow." Ella's recap of her evening with Carter astonishes Sophia. Instead of heading home, Ella needed the comfort and validation from her BFF.

"I know."

"I'm sorry, Ella. But you spoke your truth, and that's admirable. I'm sure many women might have backed down."

"It's okay. It hurts a bit, but I think deep down I knew Carter wasn't on the same page as me and that he still needed to play the field. Let's face it, our values are not in line."

"You are so mature and well-adjusted." Sophia looks at Ella sincerely.

"Yeah, thanks." Ella's tone is sarcastic. "You know what I mean."

"Men will be boys," comments Sophia as she sips on her lemon-flavored water.

"I feel like dating is like playing chess—you have to pay close attention and move strategically."

"That's because you know who you are and you're at a point where you're only going to settle for the real deal."

"I don't know about you, but I think I'm in the mood for chocolate-chocolate-chip ice cream. What do you say?" offers Sophia hoping to cheer up Ella.

"Bring it on."

"One scoop or two?"

"Definitely two."

Love Finds a Way

"Whatever our souls are made of, his and mine are the same."

~Emily Brontë

Chapter Fifteen

Throughout the following week, Ella keeps a low profile. Feeling drained of energy, she can only muster going to work and then, upon coming home, finds herself in bed early every night. Using her alone time to think, Ella goes over her life before, during, and after Jack, before, during, and after Carter, and before and after meeting and dating Harrison.

The same thoughts swim around in her head repeatedly.

Arg! Ella, please stop obsessing! You know your truth.

However, whenever she thinks of Harrison, a smile comes to her face. In fact, when she digs deep, he has always felt right.

Am I ready? I don't know. Am I afraid? Probably. Getting your heart broken is no fun.

Ella reminds herself of the C.S. Lewis quote: "To love at all is to be vulnerable."

There are no guarantees, but to live a life without love, that's even worse. Who says Harrison is going to break my heart? We can take it one day at a time. Besides, I've got you, Lord, on my side, guiding me.

In a delightful surprise, Harrison and Luke treat Sophia and Ella to a chauffeured limo ride into Manhattan for their Radio City outing. The men think of everything—from assorted beverages and catered appetizers on their ride into the city to a fantastic dinner at the famous Il Colibri Italian eatery.

After the show and dinner, Ella and Harrison stroll down Fifth Avenue behind Luke and Sophia toward the famous tree in Rockefeller Center. The magical holiday atmosphere—the stores' alluring holiday window displays, the smell of roasting chestnuts for sale, the rush of the passersby, and the attractive and festive street decorations add to the romance and excitement of an already fantastic evening.

"We'll all have to do this again." Harrison squeezes Ella's hand for emphasis.

"I'd love it."

"You would?"

"Yes," Ella replies, and without hesitation, she squeezes Harrison's hand and looks lovingly into his eyes.

Harrison intuits meaning from this gesture and look, but he wants to make sure he's reading Ella correctly. "Yes, to doing this again, or yes—*to something more?"*

"Yes, to something more. I'd like to graciously accept your offer to date exclusively, Mr. Grant."

As Rosemary expressed, after many heartfelt prayers and examination of her feelings, Ella would know her answer at the right time and place, and at this moment, Ella can be sure about her feelings for Harrison. He makes her feel cherished, secure, and protected.

Harrison stops, turns her toward him, and wraps his arms around her. "I'm so happy."

"Me, too," Ella says softly, and they kiss tenderly.

"Hey, Harrison—" Luke turns to speak to his brother and sees that he and Ella are locked in an embrace. Sophia sees it, too.

Luke laughs. "Well, look at that. They seem to be getting along quite nicely."

"I'll say," Sophia agrees.

"I'm having a great time tonight, too." Luke says, smiles warmly at Sophia.

"Oh yeah? Me too."

"Want to do this again?"

Sophia nods. "Absolutely."

"Good. Mind if I take your hand?"

"Only if you promise to give it back later." Sophia laughs.

"I'll have to think about that." Luke grins as he grabs Sophia's hand.

On Christmas Eve, Ella, Harrison, and Ella's family stand in the doorway of her parents' home, listening to neighborhood carolers sing "Joy to the World" and several other well-loved Christmas songs. The evening is warm and clear for a winter night, and the moon and stars glitter in the night sky like diamonds.

Later that evening after dinner and exchanging presents, while Julie and Tom sit chatting with Justin and Heather and Ella's parents make hot chocolate in the kitchen, Ella and Harrison make their way to the sunroom to view the twinkling night sky over the bay.

"I just love my necklace and earring set, Harrison," Ella says. She holds out the chain so she can see the beautiful, heart-shaped ruby pendant encircled with diamonds that hangs around her neck. On her ears, matching ruby and diamond stud earrings sparkle.

"They look beautiful on you." Harrison gently caresses Ella's hand. "And I love my watch. It's the perfect gift for me. I needed a new water-resistant watch for when I sail, and this suits me." He glances at his wrist around which he's wearing a new ebony watch with a black dial and white numbers. "This has got to be the best Christmas Eve ever."

"Really?"

"You're the best present a man could ever want."

Ella sighs. "Oh, Harrison." She places a hand on his shoulder. "I'm so happy."

"Me, too. I love you, Ella."

"I love you too."

Harrison pulls Ella close, and they kiss.

"This is my best Christmas Eve, ever, too." Ella smiles lovingly repeating Harrison's sentiment moments earlier as he pulls her once more.

"Merry Christmas!" Ella and Harrison greet Rosemary loudly with big smiles when she opens her front door the following morning after Christmas services.

"Merry Christmas to you both. Welcome." Ella and Rosemary kiss each other on the cheek after Ella introduces Harrison.

"I'd shake your hand, but—"chuckles Harrison.

"Oh, my, I see Santa's made another visit," laughs Rosemary. Ella holds a large bowl filled with fruit salad in one hand and a bag filled with Christmas gifts over her right arm while Harrison holds a plate of brownies and another overflowing bag of presents.

"Please come inside." Rosemary relieves Ella and Harrison of their gift bags and places them by the Christmas tree as Ella and Harrison head toward the dining room table, where they deposit their food items next to the delectable goodies Rosemary has prepared.

"I'm so glad to meet you, Harrison."

"The pleasure is mine."

"The house looks lovely," Ella says admiringly. "You've outdone yourself with all the beautiful holiday décor." The lights on Rosemary's Christmas tree, combined with holiday decorations—garland, greenery with red bows strategically placed around the glowing hearth, and a burning Yule log video with soft holiday instrumentals playing on the television—create a festive and celebratory environment. "Do you need help in the kitchen?"

"I set everything up yesterday afternoon and evening before midnight services. Once the boys and their families arrive, we can lay out the buffet. However, right now we're good to go, and we can relax and savor the morning until everyone else gets here."

Later, after Timmy, Charlie, and Adam arrive with their families, Rosemary has a private conversation with Ella in the kitchen.

"Harrison's quite a gentleman," Rosemary says.

"You said I would know when it was right, and it feels so right, Rosemary.

"The ruby necklace and earrings are just beautiful." Rosemary touches Ella's ruby heart.

"Last night, he told me he loved me, and I told him the same."

"I'm so happy for you both, dear. What a blessing and a gift."

"I know—the best gift ever."

"Wasn't that one of your Christmas wishes?"

Ella sighs and, with a nod, grasps the ruby heart.

"The man upstairs loves you, too, and so do I." Ella and Rosemary embrace.

"Will we be eating soon?" calls Timmy from the great room moments later.

Rosemary smiles. "Growing boys," she says, and Ella chuckles. "Coming, coming!"

Rosemary and Ella hurry to lay out the rest of the brunch buffet, then invite everyone to take a plate and help themselves.

"What a treat," Timmy's mother gushes before she takes a forkful of spinach quiche. "I didn't eat anything this morning, Rosemary, because Timmy told me you were preparing a feast."

"Well, I hope you all brought your appetites. Whatever we don't finish will go home in care packages."

"Does that mean we can take home all the uneaten gingerbread cookies?" asks Charlie.

Rosemary laughs. "That's precisely what it means."

"Hey, Miss Ella." Adam looks up from his plate. "I saw a flyer at the library. It has dates when you'll be reading to the local elementary school classes."

"That's right. It's something I've been doing for a while."

"Do you think I could come to one of the readings and help?"

"You would like that?" asks Ella, surprised. She can't help but smile at Adam's eagerness, his eyes shining with a newfound interest in reading.

"Yeah. I think I like reading now. I didn't use to, but after doing our essays for Miss Rosemary, well, I've come to see the value in books." Adam speaks like a mature adult. Ella has to bite her tongue not to laugh. *How adorable.*

Ella turns to Rosemary, who winks and flashes a thumbs up.

"Well, that would be wonderful, Adam. I'd love to have you read with me."

"Hey, what about us?" Timmy chimes in.

"Yeah," adds Charlie.

"Of course, I could use all your help. As upperclassmen, you'll set a wonderful example for the little ones. How about this? Let's talk after the holidays, and I'll put together a schedule. And maybe—" Ella thinks for a moment. "Maybe there's a way the school's librarian, Miss Doris, can work out special school credit for your help. It couldn't hurt to ask."

"Awesome!" yells Adam. The boys raise their hands in the air and high-five one another.

Later, after brunch, the boys and their respective siblings sit playing checkers, and Rosemary and the other adults converse amongst themselves. Ella, sitting on the sofa next to Harrison, quietly looks around the room and marvels at how, through out of something negative like the boys disrupting Rosemary's nativity display, such a loving gathering could eventually transpire. She marvels at the boys transformation in such a positive fashion.

It's all about the power of love, understanding, and forgiveness.

Then Ella remembers a passage from Ephesians 4:32: "Be kind to one another, compassionate, forgiving one another as God has forgiven you in Christ."

Christmas is definitely the season of miracles.

Unexpectedly, Harrison notices Ella is overcome with emotion. "Are you okay?" He asks, concerned.

Ella nods. "I never believed I could be as happy as I am now."

Harrison pulls Ella close and kisses her forehead. Across the room, while the others are unaware of the tender moment between Ella and Harrison, Rosemary catches a peek at the lovers and smiles.

A Merry Christmas, indeed.

Angels we have heard on high

Sweetly singing o'er the plains

"Do not neglect hospitality, for through it, some have unknowingly entertained angels."

(Hebrews 13:2)

Chapter Sixteen

Later that evening, after celebrating Christmas Day with Harrison, including a special dinner that allowed her to get to know his parents, Ella is pleasantly exhausted. Curled up and holding hands with Harrison on her great room sofa, the couple watch a rerun of *It's a Wonderful Life.*

"I believe someone I love is tired," Harrison teases when he sees Ella can't stop yawning.

"I'm sorry." Ella chuckles and rubs her eyes.

"Better get thee to bed, my dear." Harrison kisses Ella's forehead. "I'll call you in the morning. We'll figure out what we're doing for New Year's Eve. I can't wait to see what adventures await us." Harrison voice carries a definite hint of excitement.

"*Adventures?* I'm game," Ella playfully replies.

Harrison envelops Ella in a warm, tight embrace at the front door, and after one last lingering kiss, he departs for home, leaving Ella with a sense of his love and warmth.

Retiring to bed after she washes and changes into her PJs, Ella slips under the covers, her eyes heavy.

"Thank you, Lord, for all your blessings and answering my prayer. I love you so much." Moments later, Ella drifts into a deep, peaceful sleep, feeling content and grateful for the day's blessings.

In her dream, Ella is outside in her front yard headed toward Rosemary's house. It's a warm sunny day, although snow still covers the ground. The holiday decorations on Rosemary's porch glimmer like shinning stars illuminated by the sun's brilliant rays.

She feels a cool breeze caress her hair, and a distinctive, sweet aroma of red roses fills her senses.

Suddenly, Rosemary appears before Ella, dressed in the pretty white satin gown and blue shawl she wore the night of the gala. A beautiful golden light surrounds Rosemary and she looks years younger. "Harrison's a good man. I'm so happy for you, dear," says Rosemary lovingly. "Tell the boys I am proud of them and remind them how much I love them," Ella knows Rosemary refers to watching over Adam, Timmy, and Charlie.

"Are you going somewhere?"

"To tend to others in need, but I'll always keep watch over you."

"But—"

Rosemary raises her arms toward heaven, transforming into the most glorious vision ascending on high. "My soul glorifies the Lord, and my spirit rejoices in God, my Savior. Holy is His Name."

Ella wakes with a start and looks around her room to get her bearings after such an intense dream. She inhales deeply and sniffs, still smelling fragrant roses. A tingling sensation permeates her being. A second later, she turns her head toward her nightstand clock and notes the time: 9:00 a.m., way past her usual 6:00 a.m. rising. She flings back the covers and heads toward her bathroom to wash and dress.

Sipping her first cup of coffee and enjoying one of Rosemary's muffins, Ella notices a "For Sale" sign on Rosemary's lawn. *"What?"* She bolts out of her chair and heads toward the front hall closet, pulls on her long wool coat, and in seconds she's out the door.

"Excuse me, excuse me." Ella nervously approaches a woman exiting her Lexus in Rosemary's driveway. "Is Rosemary selling this house?"

"Rosemary?"

"Rosemary Engle. The woman who lives here."

"There's no such person here, Miss. Who are you, if I might ask?"

"I'm Ella Martin. I live next door." She points to her house.

"I'm Carol Winter with Brookside Realty."

Suddenly, Ella notices there's no manger on Rosemary's front lawn and no holiday decorations gracing the front porch and windows. She's baffled. "I don't understand. Rosemary came over to my house yesterday, and I've been inside her place many times."

"Look, if you want, I'll take you inside. I'm showing the house in about twenty minutes, but there's no Rosemary, no furniture. The last people to live here were the Robinsons—"

"I know, and they moved to Florida."

"Correct, *and the house is empty.*" Carol, seeing that Ella looks confused and distraught says, "Would you like to see for yourself?"

Ella follows Carol inside; sure enough, there is no furniture or sign of Rosemary.

"Okay, well, thank you." Ella's voice tone is uneasy as she heads toward home, leaving the mystery hanging in the air.

As Ella approaches her front porch, she notices a gift-wrapped package on the table next to her door. An envelope rests on top. Inside, is a two-line note that reads:

> *Do not neglect hospitality, for through it, some have unknowingly entertained angels.* –Hebrews 13:2

When Ella opens the package, she lets out an audible gasp, and a surge of electricity courses through her body. It is a gorgeous painting—a woman transported mid-air. The young woman's face is lovely and radiant, and the face is *Rosemary's*—the way Rosemary appeared the previous night in Ella's dream—surrounded by angels and cherubim ascending toward heaven.

About The Author

Photo of Maryann Ridini Spencer by Maria Gregorio-Oviedo

Maryann Ridini Spencer

Maryann Ridini Spencer pens award-winning novels and produces critically acclaimed projects for film and TV that entertain, inspire, educate, and uplift. She began her career as a producer/writer for CNN. Later, she was appointed Director of Publicity for Miss Universe, Inc. and served as Senior VP of Stephen J. Cannell Productions before founding the PR/Production company Ridini Entertainment Corporation. Maryann is also a partner in the PR/marketing company MPowerMedia, located in Rancho Mirage, California.

A member of the Writers Guild of America West and Producers Guild of America, Maryann has produced numerous movies and television series for such networks as Showtime, SyFy, TMC, USA Networks, CBS-TV, Time Warner Cable, and the foreign theatrical market. She is celebrated for co-producing/writing the teleplay for the Hallmark Hall of Fame movie *The Lost Valentine*. Based on the James Michael Pratt novel, the movie stars Betty White and Jennifer Love

Hewitt. Over fifteen million viewers tuned in to watch the film, winning CBS-TV ratings night. The film won the Faith and Freedom Movieguide® Award for inspiring American values and ideals at the nationally televised, star-studded 20th Annual Movieguide® Awards and has since become part of Hallmark's Gold Crown (DVD) Collector's Edition. It can also be live-streamed on Hallmark's movie channels.

Maryann is also the creator, writer, producer, and host of the Telly award-winning healthy living cooking series, cookbooks, and online blog magazine, *Simply Delicious Living with Maryann®*. The series and blog showcase simply delicious, easy-to-make, healthy recipes and joyous living inspirations. The series broadcasts on PBS-TV television's KVCR in Southern California, DirecTV, Dish Network, Maryann's SimplyDeliciousLiving.com blog, and to a global audience on YouTube (youtube.com/MaryannRidiniSpencer).

As a journalist, Maryann has served as a food, health, and lifestyle writer and contributing editor for *Palm Springs Life Magazine, Desert Magazine, Ventura County Star,* and *Los Angeles Magazine.*

Maryann is also the author of the *Simply Delicious Living with Maryann®—Entrées* cookbook and the award-winning, best-selling Kate Grace novels, which provide a captivating blend of romance and mystery (*Lady in the Window, The Paradise Table, Secrets of Grace Manor,* and *Under the Tropical Skies*). *Lavender Hill Cove*, the first book in Maryann's new *Lavender Hill Cove* novel series, was recently honored with a 2024 Book Excellence Award for Christian Fiction.

Visit Maryann at:
https://www.MaryannRidiniSpencer.com

And her Amazon author page:
https://www.amazon.com/stores/Maryann-Ridini-Spencer/author/B06XBHH6YK

ONCE UPON A COVE CHRISTMAS

Reader Discussion Guide

- How do you celebrate Christmas? What are your favorite holiday activities and traditions?

- Matthew 7:7-8 states: *"Seek and you will find; knock, and the door will be opened to you. For everyone who asks, receives; and the one who seeks, finds; and to the one who knocks, the door will be opened."* Can you relate this scripture to your life?

- In Chapter Four, after Carter Huxley, Ella's former boyfriend, sees Ella again and slips her a note mentioning he'd like to talk to her, he later asks her to dinner. What are your thoughts regarding Carter's attempt to reunite with Ella? Who do you think makes the better partner for Ella—Carter or Harrison and why?

- Mr. Scrooge in Charles Dicken's "A Christmas Carol" goes through a transformation when he is shown his past, present, and probable future. Have you had, or do you know, anyone who has had an experience that has caused them to change their life, direction, or attitude?

- If you had to read a book or story and write about "the deeper meaning of Christmas," what story would you choose and why?

- Describe what the deeper meaning of Christmas means for you.

- Do you believe in angels? Have you ever had an angelic experience?

- What is your favorite holiday story or movie and why?